YOUR MIND may not be much good, says the learned Dr. James Thurber, but it's all you've got to misunderstand with.

The inspirationalists are fast confusing life to that point where it will be impossible to think about something without thinking about thinking about something, and when that happens all is lost. "Wake Up and Live," they advise us. "Be Glad You're Neurotic." "Win Friends and Influence People." "Streamline Your Mind." "Live Alone and Like It."

Now James Thurber comes forward with a cheering word for the defeated. LET YOUR MIND ALONE, he counsels us. The old-fashioned technique of thinking was good enough for our fathers and should be good enough for us. The undisciplined mind, as against the disciplined or streamlined mind, has distinct and comforting advantages.

The present volume includes also such masterpieces as "The Breaking Up of the Winships," "My Memories of D. H. Lawrence," "Suli Suli," in which the author fearlessly confesses his relations with Abercrombie & Fitch, and "The Case Against Women," Which is in the nature of intimate revelation.

Bateman Comes Home

Let Your Mind Alone

AND OTHER MORE OR LESS INSPIRATIONAL

PIECES By JAMES THURBER

WITH DRAWINGS BY THE AUTHOR

The Universal Library GROSSET & DUNLAP

NEW YORK

FOR HELEN

¶ The essays and stories in this book were originally printed in *The New Yorker*, with the exception of "After the Steppe Cat, What?", which appeared in *The Forum*, and "Women Go On Forever," which appeared in *For Men Only*.

CONTENTS

Part One

Let your mind alone!

1. Pythagoras and the Ladder

IT WAS IN NONE OTHER THAN THE BLACK, MEMORABLE YEAR 1929 that the indefatigable Professor Walter B. Pitkin rose up with the announcement that "for the first time in the career of mankind happiness is coming within the reach of millions of people." Happy living, he confidently asserted, could be attained by at least six or seven people out of every ten, but he figured that not more than one person in a thousand was actually attaining it. However, all the external conditions required for happy living were present, he said, just waiting to be used. The only obstacle was a psychological one. Figuring on a basis of 130,000,000 population in this country and reducing the Professor's estimates to round numbers, we find that in 1929 only 130,000 people were happy, but that between 78,000,000 and 91,000,000 could have been happy, leaving only 52,000,000, at the outside, doomed to discontent. The trouble with all the unhappy ones (except the 52,000,000) was that they didn't Know Themselves, they didn't understand the Science of Happiness, they had no Technique of Thinking. Professor Pitkin wrote a book on the subject; he is, in fact, always writing a book on the subject. So are a number of other people. I have devoted myself to a careful study of as many of these books as a man of my unsteady eyesight and wandering attention could be expected to encompass. And I decided to write a series of articles of my own on the subject, examining what the Success Experts have to say and offering some ideas of my own, the basic one of which is, I think, that man will be better

3

Conducting a Lady to a Table in a Restaurant

off if he quits monkeying with his mind and just lets it alone. In this, the first of the series, I shall abandon Professor Pitkin to his percentages and his high hopes and consider the author of a best-seller published last summer (an alarming number of these books reach the best-seller list). Let us plunge right into Dr. James L. Mursell's "Streamline Your Mind" and see what he has to contribute to the New Happiness, as Professor Pitkin has called it.

In Chapter VI, which is entitled "Using What You've Got," Dr. Mursell deals with the problem of how to learn and how to make use of what you have learned. He believes, to begin with, that you should learn things by doing them, not by just reading up on them. In this connection he presents the case of a young man who wanted to find out "how to conduct a lady to a table in a restaurant." Although I have been gored by a great many dilemmas in my time, that particular problem doesn't happen to have been one of them. I must have just stumbled onto the way to conduct a lady to a table in a restaurant. I don't remember, as a young man, ever having given the matter much thought, but I know that I frequently worried about whether I would have enough money to pay for the dinner and still tip the waiter. Dr. Mursell does not touch on the difficult problem of how to maintain your poise as you depart from a restaurant table on which you have left no tip. I constantly find these mental authorities avoiding the larger issues in favor of something which seems comparatively trivial. The plight of the Doctor's young man, for instance, is as nothing compared to my own plight one time in a restaurant in Columbus when I looked up to find my cousin Wilmer Thurber standing beside me flecked with buttermilk and making a sound which was something between the bay of a beagle and the cry of a large bird.

I had been having lunch in the outer of two small rooms

which comprised a quiet basement restaurant known as the Hole in the Wall, opposite the State House grounds, a place much frequented by elderly clerks and lady librarians, in spite of its raffish name. Wilmer, it came out, was in the other room; neither of us knew the other was there. The Hole in the Wall was perhaps the calmest restaurant I have ever known; the studious people who came there for lunch usually lunched alone; you rarely heard anybody talk. The aged proprietor of the place, because of some defect, spoke always in whispers, and this added to an effect of almost monasterial quiet. It was upon this quiet that there fell suddenly, that day, the most unearthly sound I have ever heard. My back was to the inner room and I was too disconcerted to look around. But from the astonished eyes of those who sat in front of me facing the doorway to that room I became aware that the Whatever-It-Was had entered our room and was approaching my table. It wasn't until a cold hand was laid on mine that I looked up and beheld Wilmer, who had, it came out, inhaled a draught of buttermilk as one might inhale cigarette smoke, and was choking. Having so fortunately found me, he looked at me with wide, stricken eyes and, still making that extraordinary sound, a low, canine *how-ooo* that rose to a high, birdlike *yeee-eep*, he pointed to the small of his back as who should say "Hit me!" There I was, faced with a restaurant problem which, as I have said, makes that of Dr. Mursell's young man seem very unimportant indeed. What I did finally, after an awful, frozen moment, was to get up and dash from the place, without even paying for my lunch. I sent the whispering old man a check, but I never went back to his restaurant. Many of our mental authorities, most of whom are psychologists of one school or another, will say that my dreadful experience must have implanted in me a fear of restaurants (Restauphobia). It did nothing of the sort; it simply implanted in me a wariness of

Wilmer. I never went into a restaurant after that without first making sure that this inveterate buttermilk-drinker was not there.

But let us get back to Dr. Mursell and his young man's peculiar quandary. I suppose this young man must have got to worrying about who went first, the lady or himself. These things, as we know, always work out; if the young man doesn't work them out, the lady will. (If she wants him to go first, she will say, "You go first.") What I am interested in here is not the correct procedure but Dr. Mursell's advice to the young man in question. He writes, "Do not merely learn it in words. Try it over with your sister." In that second sentence he reveals, it seems to me, what these inspirationalists so frequently reveal, a lack of understanding of people; in this case, brothers and sisters. Ninety-nine brothers out of a hundred who were worrying about how to conduct a lady to a table in a restaurant would starve before they would go to their sisters and ask them how the thing is done. They would as lief go to their mothers and have a good, frank talk about sex. But let us, for the sake of the argument, try Dr. Mursell's system.

Sister, who is twenty-one, and who goes around with a number of young men whom her brother frankly regards as pussy-cats, is sitting by the fire one evening reading André Gide, or *Photoplay*, or something. Brother, who is eighteen, enters. "Where's Mom?" he asks. "How should I know?" she snaps. "Thought you might know that, Stupid. Y'ought to know something," he snaps back. Sister continues to read, but she is obviously annoyed by the presence of her brother; he is chewing gum, making a strange, cracking noise every fifth chew, and this gets on her nerves. "Why don't you spit out that damn gum?" she asks, finally. "Aw, nuts," says her brother, in a falsetto singsong. "Nuts to you, Baby, nuts." There is a long, tense silence; he rustles and re-rustles the evening paper. "Where's Itsy Bitsy Dicky tonight?" he asks, suddenly. "Ditch you for a live gal?" By Itsy Bitsy Dicky, he refers to one Richard Warren, a beau of his sister's, whom he considers a hollyhock. "Why don't you go to hell?" asks his sister, coldly. Brother reads the sports page and begins to whistle "Horses," a song which has annoyed his sister since she was ten and he was seven, and which he is whistling for that reason. "*Stop* that!" she screams, at last. He stops for about five seconds and then bursts out, loudly, "*Cra*-zy over *hor*-ses, *hor*-ses, *hor*-ses, she's a little wi-i-i-ld!" Here we have, I think, a typical meeting between brother and sister. Now, out of it, somehow, we have to arrive at a *tableau vivant* in which the brother asks the sister to show him how to conduct a lady to a table in a restaurant. Let us attempt to work that out. "Oh, say, Sis," the brother begins, after a long pause. "Shut up, you lout!" she says. "No, listen, I want to ask you a favor." He begins walking around the room, blushing. "I've asked Greta Dearing out to dinner tomorrow night and I'm not sure how to get her to the table. I mean whether—I mean I don't know how we both get to the table. Come on out in the hall with me and we'll pretend this room is the restaurant. You show me how to get you over to that table in the corner." The note of falsity is so apparent in this that I need not carry out the embarrassing fiction any longer. Obviously the young man is going to have to read up on the subject or, what is much simpler, just take his girl to the restaurant. This acting-out of things falls down of its own stuffiness.

There is a curious tendency on the part of the How-to-Live men to make things hard. It recurs time and again in the thought-technique books. In this same Chapter VI there is a classic example of it. Dr. Mursell recounts the remarkable experience of a professor and his family who were faced with the necessity of reroofing their country house. They decided, for some obscure reason, to do the work themselves, and they intended to order the materials from Sears, Roebuck. The first thing, of course, was to find out how much roofing material they needed. "Here," writes Dr. Mursell, "they struck a snag." They didn't, he points out, have a ladder, and since the roof was too steep to climb, they were at their wits' end as to how they were going to go about measuring it. You and I have this problem solved already: we would get a ladder. But not, it wonderfully turns out, Dr. Mursell's professor and his family. "For several days," writes Dr. Mursell, "they were completely stumped." Nobody thought of getting a ladder. It is impossible to say how they would have solved their problem had not a guest come finally to visit them. This guest noticed that the angle formed by the two sides of the roof (which were equal in length) was a right angle. Let Dr. Mursell go on, in his ecstatic way, from there. "An isosceles right-angled triangle with the base of known length! Had nobody ever been told that the sum of the squares on the two sides of such a triangle was equal to the square of the hypotenuse? And couldn't anyone do a little arithmetic? How very simple! One could easily figure the measurements for the sides of the roof, and as the length of the house could be found without any climbing, the area could be discovered. The theorem of Pythagoras could be used in place of the ladder."

I think this places Dr. James L. Mursell for you; at any rate it does for me: he is the man who would use the theorem of Pythagoras in place of a ladder. I keep wondering what would have happened if that guest hadn't turned up, or if he had remembered the theorem of Pythagoras the way many people do: the sum of the squares of the two sides of a right-angled triangle is equal to *twice* the sum of the hypotenuse, or some other such variant. Many a person, doing a little arithmetic in this case, would order enough material from

Sears, Roebuck to roof seven houses. It seems to me that borrowing a ladder from next door, or buying one from a hardware store, is a much simpler way to go about measuring a roof than waiting for somebody to show up who knows the theorem of Pythagoras. Most people who show up at my house can't remember anything they learned in school except possibly the rule for compound Latin verbs that take the dative. My roof would never be fixed; it would rain in; probably I'd have to sell the house, at a great loss, to somebody who has a ladder. With a ladder of my own, and the old-fashioned technique of thinking, I could get the job done in no time. This seems to me the simplest way to live.

2. Destructive Forces in Life

THE MENTAL EFFICIENCY BOOKS GO INTO ELABORATE DETAIL about how to attain Masterful Adjustment, as one of them calls it, but it seems to me that the problems they set up, and knock down, are in the main unimaginative and pedestrian: the little fusses at the breakfast table, the routine troubles at the office, the familiar anxieties over money and health—the welter of workaday annoyances which all of us meet with and usually conquer without extravagant wear and tear. Let us examine, as a typical instance, a brief case history presented by the learned Mr. David Seabury, author of "What Makes Us Seem So Queer," "Unmasking Our Minds," "Keep Your Wits," "Growing Into Life," and "How to Worry Successfully." I select it at random. "Frank Fulsome," writes Mr. Seabury, "flung down the book with disgust and growled an insult at his wife. That little lady put her hands to her face and fled from the room. She was sure Frank must hate her to speak so cruelly. Had she known it, he was not really speaking to her at all. The occasion merely gave vent to a pent-up desire to 'punch his fool boss in the jaw.'" This is, I believe, a characteristic Seabury situation. Many of the women in his treatises remind you of nobody so much as Ben Bolt's Alice, who "wept with delight when you gave her a smile, and trembled with fear at your frown." The little ladies most of us know would, instead of putting their hands to their faces and fleeing from the room, come right back at Frank Fulsome. Frank would perhaps be lucky if he didn't get a punch in the jaw himself. In any case, the situation would be cleared up in approximately three minutes. This "had she known" business is not as common among wives today as Mr. Seabury seems to think it is. The Latent Content (as the psychologists call it) of a husband's mind is usually as clear to the wife as the Manifest Content, frequently much clearer.

I could cite a dozen major handicaps to Masterful Adjustment which the thought technicians never touch upon, a dozen

A Mentally Disciplined Husband with Mentally Undisciplined Wife

situations not so easy of analysis and solution as most of theirs. I will, however, content myself with one. Let us consider the case of a man of my acquaintance who had accomplished Discipline of Mind, overcome the Will to Fail, mastered the Technique of Living—had, in a word, practically attained Masterful Adjustment—when he was called on the phone one afternoon about five o'clock by a man named Bert Scursey. The other man, whom I shall call Harry Conner, did not answer the phone, however; his wife answered it. As Scursey told me the story later, he had no intention when he dialled the Conners' apartment at the Hotel Graydon of doing more than talk with Harry. But, for some strange reason, when Louise Conner answered, Bert Scursey found himself pretending to be, and imitating the voice of, a colored woman. This Scursey is by way of being an excellent mimic, and a colored woman is one of the best things he does.

"Hello," said Mrs. Conner. In a plaintive voice, Scursey said, "Is dis heah Miz Commah?" "Yes, this is Mrs. Conner," said Louise. "Who is speaking?" "Dis heah's Edith Rummum," said Scursey. "Ah used wuck fo yo frens was nex doah yo place a Sou Norwuck." Naturally, Mrs. Conner did not follow this, and demanded rather sharply to know who was calling and what she wanted. Scursey, his voice soft with feigned tears, finally got it over to his friend's wife that he was one Edith Rummum, a colored maid who had once worked for some friends of the Conners' in South Norwalk, where they had lived some years before. "What is it you want, Edith?" asked Mrs. Conner, who was completely taken in by the imposter (she could not catch the name of the South Norwalk friends, but let that go). Scursey—or Edith, rather —explained in a pitiable, hesitant way that she was without work or money and that she didn't know what she was going to do; Rummum, she said, was in the jailhouse because of a cutting scrape on a roller-coaster. Now, Louise Conner happened to be a most kind-hearted person, as Scursey well knew, so she said that she could perhaps find some laundry work for Edith to do. "Yessum," said Edith. "Ah laundas." At this point, Harry Conner's voice, raised in the room behind his wife, came clearly to Scursey, saying, "Now, for God's sake, Louise, don't go giving our clothes out to somebody you never saw or heard of in your life." This interjection of Conner's was in firm keeping with a theory of logical behavior which he had got out of the Mind and Personality books. There was no Will to Weakness here, no Desire to

Have His Shirts Ruined, no False Sympathy for the Colored Woman Who Has Not Organized Her Life.

But Mrs. Conner who often did not listen to Mr. Conner, in spite of his superior mental discipline, prevailed.* "Where are you now, Edith?" she asked. This disconcerted Scursey for a moment, but he finally said, "Ah's jes rounda corna, Miz Commah." "Well, you come over to the Hotel Graydon," said Mrs. Conner. "We're in Apartment 7-A on the seventh floor." "Yessm," said Edith. Mrs. Conner hung up and so did Scursey. He was now, he realized, in something of a predicament. Since he did not possess a streamlined mind, as Dr. Mursell has called it, and had definitely a Will to Confuse, he did not perceive that his little joke had gone far enough. He wanted to go on with it, which is a characteristic of woolgatherers, pranksters, wags, wish-fulfillers, and escapists generally. He enjoyed fantasy as much as reality, probably even more, which is a sure symptom of Regression, Digression, and Analogical Redintegration. What he finally did, therefore, was to call back the Conners and get Mrs. Conner on the phone again. "Jeez, Miz Commah," he said, with a hint of panic in his voice, "Ah cain' fine yo apottoman!" "Where are you, Edith?" she asked. "Lawd, Ah doan know," said Edith. "Ah's on *some* floah in de Hotel Graydon." "Well, listen, Edith, you took the elevator, didn't you?" "Dass whut Ah took," said Edith, uncertainly. "Well, you go back to the elevator and tell the boy you want off at the seventh floor. I'll meet you at the elevator." "Yessm," said Edith, with even more uncertainty. At this point, Conner's loud voice, speaking to his wife, was again heard by Scursey. "Where in the hell is she calling from?" demanded Conner, who had developed Logical Reasoning. "She must have wandered into somebody else's apart-

* This sometimes happens even when the husband is mentally disciplined and the wife is not.

ment if she is calling you from this building, for God's sake!" Whereupon, having no desire to explain where Edith was calling from, Scursey hung up.

After an instant of thought, or rather Disintegrated Phantasmagoria, Scursey rang the Conners again. He wanted to prevent Louise from going out to the elevator and checking up with the operator. This time, as Scursey had hoped, Harry Conner answered, having told his wife that he would handle this situation. "Hello!" shouted Conner, irritably. "Who is this?" Scursey now abandoned the rôle of Edith and assumed a sharp, fussy, masculine tone. "Mr. Conner," he said, crisply, "this is the office. I am afraid we shall have to ask you to remove this colored person from the building. She is blundering into other people's apartments, using their phones. We cannot have that sort of thing, you know, at the Graydon." The man's words and his tone infuriated Conner. "There are a lot of sort of things I'd like to see you not have at the Graydon!" he shouted. "Well, please come down to the lobby and do something about this situation," said the man, nastily. "You're damned right I'll come down!" howled Conner. He banged down the receiver.

Bert Scursey sat in a chair and gloated over the involved state of affairs which he had created. He decided to go over to the Graydon, which was just up the street from his own apartment, and see what was happening. It promised to have all the confusion which his disorderly mind so deplorably enjoyed. And it did have. He found Conner in a tremendous rage in the lobby, accusing an astonished assistant manager of having insulted him. Several persons in the lobby watched the curious scene. "But, Mr. Conner," said the assistant manager, a Mr. Bent, "I have no idea what you are talking about." "If you listen, you'll find out!" bawled Harry Conner. "In the first place, this colored woman's coming to the hotel was no idea of mine. I've never seen her in my life and I don't want to see her! I want to go to my *grave* without seeing her!" He had forgotten what the Mind and Personality books had taught him: never raise your voice in anger, always stick to the point. Naturally, Mr. Bent could only believe that his guest had gone out of his mind. He decided to humor him. "Where is this—ah—colored woman, Mr. Conner?" he asked, warily. He was somewhat pale and was fiddling with a bit of paper. A dabbler in psychology books himself, he knew that colored women are often Sex Degradation symbols, and he wondered if Conner had not fallen out of love with his wife without realizing it. (This theory, I believe, Mr. Bent has clung to ever since, although the Conners are one of the happiest couples in the country). "I don't know where she is!" cried Conner. "She's up on some other floor phoning my wife! *You* seemed to know all about it! I had nothing to do with it! I opposed it from the start! But I want no insults from you no matter *who* opposed it!" "Certainly not, certainly not," said Mr. Bent, backing slightly away. He began to wonder what he was going to do with this maniac.

At this juncture Scursey, who had been enjoying the scene at a safe distance, approached Conner and took him by the arm. "What's the matter, old boy?" he asked. "H'lo, Bert," said Conner, sullenly. And then, his eyes narrowing, he began to examine the look on Scursey's face. Scursey is not good at dead-panning; he is only good on the phone. There was a guilty grin on his face. "You ———," said Conner, bitterly, remembering Scursey's pranks of mimicry, and he turned on his heel, walked to the elevator, and, when Scursey tried to get in too, shoved him back into the lobby. That was the end of the friendship between the Conners and Bert Scursey. It was more than that. It was the end of Harry Conner's stay at the Graydon. It was, in fact, the end of his stay in New

York City. He and Louise live in Oregon now, where Conner accepted a less important position than he had held in New York because the episode of Edith had turned him against Scursey, Mr. Bent, the Graydon, and the whole metropolitan area.

Anybody can handle the Frank Fulsomes of the world, but is there anything to be done about the Bert Scurseys? Can we so streamline our minds that the antics of the Scurseys roll off them like water off a duck's back? I don't think so. I believe the authors of the inspirational books don't think so, either, but are afraid to attack the subject. I imagine they have been hoping nobody would bring it up. Hardly anybody goes through life without encountering his Bert Scursey and having his life—and his mind—accordingly modified. I have known a dozen Bert Scurseys. I have often wondered what happened to some of their victims. There was, for example, the man who rang up a waggish friend of mine by mistake, having got a wrong number. "Is this the Shu-Rite Shoestore?" the caller asked, querulously. "Shu-Rite Shoestore, good morning!" said my friend, brightly. "Well," said the other, "I just called up to say that the shoes I bought there a week ago are shoddy. They're made, by God, of cardboard. I'm going to bring them in and show you. I want satisfaction!" "And you shall have it!" said my friend. "Our shoes are, as you say, shoddy. There have been many complaints, many complaints. Our shoes, I am afraid, simply go to pieces on the foot. We shall, of course, refund your money." I know another man who was always being roused out of bed by people calling a certain railroad which had a similar phone number. "When can I get a train to Buffalo?" a sour-voiced woman demanded one morning about seven o'clock. "Not till two A.M. tomorrow, Madam," said this man. "But that's ridiculous!" cried the woman, "I know," said the man, "and we realize that. Hence we include, in the regular fare, a taxi which will call for you in plenty of time to make the train. Where do you live?" The lady, slightly mollified, told him an address in the Sixties. "We'll have a cab there at one-thirty, Madam," he said. "The driver will handle your baggage." "Now I can count on that?" she said. "Certainly, Madam," he told her. "One-thirty, sharp."

Just what changes were brought about in that woman's character by that call, I don't know. But the thing might have altered the color and direction of her life, the pattern of her mind, the whole fabric of her nature. Thus we see that a person might build up a streamlined mind, a mind awakened to a new life, a new discipline, only to have the whole works shot to pieces by so minor and unpredictable a thing as a wrong telephone number. On the other hand, the undisciplined mind would never have the fortitude to consider a trip to Buffalo at two in the morning, nor would it have the determination to seek redress from a shoestore which had sold it a faulty pair of shoes. Hence the undisciplined mind runs far less chance of having its purposes thwarted, its plans distorted, its whole scheme and system wrenched out of line. The undisciplined mind, in short, is far better adapted to the confused world in which we live today than the streamlined mind. This is, I am afraid, no place for the streamlined mind.

3. The Case for the Daydreamer

ALL THE BOOKS IN MY EXTENSIVE LIBRARY ON TRAINING THE mind agree that realism, as against fantasy, reverie, daydreaming, and woolgathering, is a highly important thing. "Be a realist," says Dr. James L. Mursell, whose "Streamline Your Mind" I have already discussed. "Take a definite step to turn a dream into a reality," says Mrs. Dorothea Brande, the "Wake-Up-and-Live!" woman. They allow you a certain amount of reverie and daydreaming (no woolgathering), but only when it is purposeful, only when it is going to lead to realistic action and concrete achievement. In this insistence on reality I do not see as much profit as these Shapers of Success do. I have had a great deal of satisfaction and benefit out of daydreaming which never got me anywhere in their definition of getting somewhere. I am reminded, as an example, of an incident which occurred this last summer.

I had been travelling about the country attending dog shows. I was writing a series of pieces on these shows. Not being in the habit of carrying press cards, letters of introduction, or even, in some cases, the key to my car or the tickets to a show which I am on my way to attend, I had nothing by which to identify myself. I simply paid my way in, but at a certain dog show I determined to see if the officials in charge would give me a pass. I approached a large, heavy-set man who looked somewhat like Victor McLaglen. His name was Bustard. Mr. Bustard. "You'll have to see Mr. Bustard," a ticket-taker had told me. This Mr. Bustard was apparently

Child Making Flat Statements about a Gentleman's Personal Appearance

very busy trying to find bench space for old Miss Emily Van Winkle's Pomeranians, which she had entered at the last minute, and attending to a number of other matters. He glanced at me, saw that he outweighed me some sixty pounds, and decided to make short shrift of whatever it was I wanted. I explained I was writing an article about the show and would like a pass to get in. "Why, that's impossible!" he cried. "That's ridiculous! If I gave you a pass, I'd have to give a pass to everyone who came up and asked me for a pass!" I was pretty much overwhelmed. I couldn't, as is usual in these cases, think of anything to say except "I see." Mr. Bustard delivered a brief, snarling lecture on the subject of people who expect to get into dog shows free, unless they are showing dogs, and ended with "Are you showing dogs?" I tried to think of something sharp and well-turned. "No, I'm not showing any dogs," I said, coldly. Mr. Bustard abruptly turned his back on me and walked away.

As soon as Mr. Bustard disappeared, I began to think of things I should have said. I thought of a couple of sharp cracks on his name, the least pointed of which was Buzzard. Finely edged comebacks leaped to mind. Instead of going into the dog show—or following Mr. Bustard—I wandered up and down the streets of the town, improving on my retorts. I fancied a much more successful encounter with Mr. Bustard. In this fancied encounter, I, in fact, enraged Mr. Bustard. He lunged at me, whereupon, side-stepping agilely, I led with my left and floored him with a beautiful right to the jaw. "Try that one!" I cried aloud. "Mercy!" murmured an old lady who was passing me at the moment. I began to walk more rapidly; my heart took a definite lift. Some people, in my dream, were bending over Bustard, who was out cold. "Better take him home and let the other bustards pick his bones," I said. When I got back to the dog show, I was in high fettle.

After several months I still feel, when I think of Mr. Bustard, that I got the better of him. In a triumphant daydream, it seems to me, there is felicity and not defeat. You can't just take a humiliation and dismiss it from your mind, for it will crop up in your dreams, but neither can you safely carry a dream into reality in the case of an insensitive man like Mr. Bustard who outweighs you by sixty pounds. The thing to do is to visualize a triumph over the humiliator so vividly and insistently that it becomes, in effect, an actuality. I went on with my daydreams about Mr. Bustard. All that day at the dog show I played tricks on him in my imagination, I outgeneralled him, I made him look silly, I had him on the run. I would imagine myself sitting in a living room. It was late at night. Outside it was raining heavily. The doorbell rang. I went to the door and opened it, and a man was standing there. "I wonder if you would let me use your phone?" he asked. "My car has broken down." It was, of all people, Mr. Bustard. You can imagine my jibes, my sarcasm, my repartee, my shutting the door in his face at the end. After a whole afternoon of this kind of thing, I saw Mr. Bustard on my way out of the show. I actually felt a little sorry about the tossing around I had given him. I gave him an enigmatic, triumphant smile which must have worried him a great deal. He must have wondered what I had been up to, what superior of his I had seen, what I had done to get back at him—who, after all, I was.

Now, let us figure Dr. Mursell in my place. Let us suppose that Dr. Mursell went up to Mr. Bustard and asked him for a pass to the dog show on the ground that he could streamline the dog's intuition. I fancy that Mr. Bustard also outweighs Dr. Mursell by sixty pounds and is in better fighting trim; we men who write treatises on the mind are not likely to be in as good shape as men who run dog shows. Dr. Mursell, then, is rebuffed, as I was. If he tries to get back at Mr. Bustard right there and then, he will find himself saying "I see" or "Well, I didn't know" or, at best, "I just asked you." Even the streamlined mind runs into this Blockage, as the psychologists call it. Dr. Mursell, like myself, will go away and think up better things to say, but, being a realist dedicated to carrying a dream into actuality, he will perforce have to come back and tackle Mr. Bustard again. If Mr. Bustard's patience gives out, or if he is truly stung by some crack of the Doctor's he is likely to begin shoving, or snap his fingers, or say "'Raus!," or even tweak the Doctor's nose. Dr. Mursell, in that case, would get into no end of trouble. Realists are always getting into trouble. They miss the sweet, easy victories of the day-dreamer.

I do not pretend that the daydream cannot be carried too far. If at this late date, for instance, I should get myself up to look as much like Mr. Bustard as possible and then, gazing into the bathroom mirror, snarl "Bustard, you dog!," that would be carrying the daydream too far. One should never run the risk of identifying oneself with the object of one's scorn. I have no idea what complexes and neuroses might lie that way. The mental experts could tell you—or, if they couldn't, they would anyway.

Now let us turn briefly to the indomitable Mrs. Brande, eight of whose precious words of advice have, the ads for her book tell us, changed the lives of 860,000 people, or maybe it is 86,000,000—Simon & Schuster published her book. (These words are "act as if it were impossible to fail," in case your life hasn't been changed.) Discussing realistic action as against the daydream, she takes up the case of a person, any person, who dreams about going to Italy but is getting nowhere. The procedure she suggests for such a person is threefold: (1) read a current newspaper in Italian, buy some histories, phrase books, and a small grammar; (2) put aside a small coin each day; (3) do something in your spare time to make money— "if it is nothing more than to sit with children while their parents are at parties." (I have a quick picture of the parents reeling from party to party, but that is beside the point.)

I can see the newspaper and the books intensifying the dream, but I can't somehow see them getting anybody to Italy. As for putting a small coin aside each day, everybody who has tried it knows that it does not work out. At the end of three weeks you usually have $2.35 in the pig bank or the cooky jar, a dollar and a half of which you have to use for something besides Italy, such as a C.O.D. package. At that rate, all that you would have in the bank or the jar at the end of six years would be about $87.45. Within the next six years Italy will probably be at war, and even if you were well enough to travel after all that time, you couldn't get into the country. The disappointment of a dream nursed for six years, with a reality in view that did not eventuate, would be enough to embitter a person for life. As for this business of sitting with children while their parents are at parties, anybody who has done it knows that no trip to anywhere, even Utopia, would be worth it. Very few people can sit with children, especially children other than their own, more than an hour and a half without having their dispositions and even their characters badly mauled about. In fifteen minutes the average child whose parents are at a party can make enough flat statements of fact about one's personal appearance and ask enough pointed questions about one's private life to send one away feeling that there is little, if any, use in going on with anything at all, let alone a trip to Italy.

The long and hard mechanics of reality which these inspirationalists suggest are, it seems to me, far less satisfactory than the soft routine of a dream. The dreamer builds up for himself no such towering and uncertain structure of hope; he has no depleted cooky jar to shake his faith in himself. It is significant that the line "Oh, to be in England now that April's there," which is a definite dream line, is better known than any line the poet wrote about actually being in England. (I guess *that* will give the inspirationalists something to think about.) You can sit up with children if you want to, you can put a dime a day in an empty coffee tin, you can read the Fascist viewpoint in an Italian newspaper, but when it comes to a choice between the dream and the reality of present-day Italy, I personally shall sit in a corner by the fire and read "The Ring and the Book." And in the end it will probably be me who sends you a postcard from Italy, which you can put between the pages of the small grammar or the phrase book.

4. A Dozen Disciplines

Mrs. DOROTHEA BRANDE, WHOSE THEORY OF HOW TO GET TO Italy I discussed in the preceding pages, has a chapter in her "Wake Up and Live!" which suggests twelve specific disciplines. The purpose of these disciplines, she says, is to make our minds keener and more flexible. I'll take them up in order and show why it is no use for Mrs. Brande to try to sharpen and limber up my mind, if these disciplines are all she has to offer. I quote them as they were quoted in a Simon & Schuster advertisement for the book, because the advertisement puts them more succinctly than Mrs. Brande does herself.

"1. Spend one hour a day without speaking except in answer to direct questions."

No hour of the day goes by that I am not in some minor difficulty which could easily become major if I did not shout for help. Just a few hours ago, for example, I found myself in a dilemma that has become rather familiar about my house: I had got tied up in a typewriter ribbon. The whole thing had come unwound from the spool and was wound around me. What started as an unfortunate slip of the hand slowly grew into an enormous involvement. To have gone a whole hour waiting for someone to show up and ask me a question could not conceivably have improved my mind. Two minutes of silence now and then is all right, but that is as far as I will go.

"2. Think one hour a day about one subject exclusively."

Such as what, for example? At forty-two, I have spent a

great many hours thinking about all sorts of subjects, and there is not one of them that I want to go back to for a whole solid hour. I can pretty well cover as much of any subject as I want to in fifteen minutes. Sometimes in six. Furthermore, it would be impossible for me, or for Mrs. Brande, or for Simon & Schuster to think for an hour exclusively on one

American Male Tied up in Typewriter Ribbon

subject. What is known as "psychological association" would be bound to come into the thing. For instance, let us say that I decide to think for a solid hour about General Grant's horse (as good a subject as any at a time when practically all subjects are in an unsettled state). The fact that it is General Grant's horse would remind me of General Grant's beard and that would remind me of Charles Evans Hughes and that would

remind me of the NRA. And so it would go. If I resolutely
went back to General Grant's horse again, I would, by association, begin thinking about General Lee's horse, which was
a much more famous horse, a horse named Traveller. I doubt
if Mrs. Brande even knows the name of General Grant's horse,
much less enough about it to keep her mind occupied for
sixty minutes. I mean sixty minutes of real constructive thinking that would get her somewhere. Sixty minutes of thinking
of any kind is bound to lead to confusion and unhappiness.

"3. Write a letter without using the first person singular."
What for? To whom? About what? All I could possibly
think of to write would be a letter to a little boy telling him
how to build a rabbit hutch, and I don't know how to build
a rabbit hutch very well. I never knew a little boy who couldn't
tell me more about building a rabbit hutch than I could tell
him. Nobody in my family was ever good at building rabbit
hutches, although a lot of us raised rabbits. I have sometimes
wondered how we managed it. I remember the time that my
father offered to help me and my two brothers build a rabbit
hutch out of planks and close-meshed chicken wire. Somehow
or other he got inside of the cage after the wire had been put
up around the sides and over the top, and he began to monkey
with the stout door. I don't know exactly what happened, but
he shut the door and it latched securely and he was locked in
with the rabbits. The place was a shambles before he got out,
because nobody was home at the time and he couldn't get his
hand through the wire to unlatch the door. He had his derby
on in the hutch all during his captivity and that added to
his discomfiture. I remember, too, that we boys (we were not
yet in our teens) didn't at first know what the word "hutch"
meant, but we had got hold of a pamphlet on the subject,
which my brother Herman read with great care. One sentence in the pamphlet read, "The rabbits' hutches should be

cleaned thoroughly once a week." It was this admonition which caused my brother one day to get each of the astonished rabbits down in turn and wash its haunches thoroughly with soap and water.

No, I do not think that anybody can write a letter without using the first person singular. Even if it could be done, I see no reason to do it.

"4. Talk for fifteen minutes without using the first person."

No can do. No going to *try* to do, either. You can't teach an old egoist new persons.

"5. Write a letter in a placid, successful tone, sticking to facts about yourself."

Now we're getting somewhere, except that nothing is more stuffy and conceited-sounding than a "placid, successful tone." The way to write about yourself is to let yourself go. Build it up, exaggerate, make yourself out a person of importance. Fantasy is the food for the mind, not facts. Are we going to wake up and live or are we going to sit around writing factual letters in a placid, successful tone?

"6. Pause before you enter any crowded room and consider your relations with the people in it."

Now, Mrs. Brande, if I did that there would be only about one out of every thirty-two crowded rooms I approached that I would ever enter. I always shut my mind and plunge into a crowded room as if it were a cold bath. That gives me and everybody in the room a clean break, a fresh starting point. There is no good in rehashing a lot of old relations with people. The longer I paused outside a crowded room and thought about my relations with the people in it, the more inclined I would be to go back to the checkroom and get my hat and coat and go home. That's the best place for a person, anyway—home.

"7. Keep a new acquaintance talking, exclusively about himself."

And then tiptoe quietly away. He'll never notice the difference.

"8. Talk exclusively about yourself for fifteen minutes."

And see what happens.

"9. Eliminate the phrases 'I mean' and 'As a matter of fact' from your conversation."

Okie-dokie.

"10. Plan to live two hours a day according to a rigid time schedule."

Well, I usually wake up at nine in the morning and lie there till eleven, if that would do. Of course, I could *plan* to do a lot of different things over a period of two hours, but if I actually started out to accomplish them I would instantly begin to worry about whether I was going to come out on the dot in the end and I wouldn't do any of them right. It would be like waiting for the pistol shot during the last quarter of a close football game. This rule seems to me to be devised simply to make men irritable and jumpy.

"11. Set yourself twelve instructions on pieces of paper, shuffle them, and follow the one you draw. Here are a few samples: 'Go twelve hours without food.' 'Stay up all night and work.' 'Say nothing all day except in answer to questions.'"

In that going twelve hours without food, do you mean I can have drinks? Because if I can have drinks, I can do it easily. As for staying up all night and working, I know all about that: that simply turns night into day and day into night. I once got myself into such a state staying up all night that I was always having orange juice and boiled eggs at twilight and was just ready for lunch after everybody had gone to bed. I had to go away to a sanitarium to get turned around. As for saying nothing all day except in answer to questions, what am I to do if a genial colleague comes into my office and says, "I think your mother is one of the nicest people I ever met" or "I was thinking about giving you that twenty dollars you lent me"? Do I just stare at him and walk out of the room? I lose enough friends, and money, the way it is.

"12. Say 'Yes' to every reasonable request made of you in the course of one day."

All right, start making some. I can't think of a single one offhand. The word "reasonable" has taken a terrible tossing around in my life—both personal and business. If you mean watering the geraniums, I'll do that. If you mean walking around Central Park with you for the fresh air and exercise, you are crazy.

Has anybody got any more sets of specific disciplines? If anybody has, they've got to be pretty easy ones if I am going to wake up and live. It's mighty comfortable dozing here and waiting for the end.

5. How to Adjust Yourself to Your Work

I FIND THAT THE INSPIRATIONAL BOOKS ARE FREQUENTLY DISposed to touch, with pontifical cheerfulness or owlish mysticism, on the problem of how to get along in the business world, how to adjust yourself to your employer and to your fellow-worker. It seems to me that in this field the trainers of the mind, both lady and gentleman, are at their unhappiest. Let us examine, in this our fourth lesson, what Mrs. Dorothea Brande, who is reputedly changing the lives of almost as many people as the Oxford Group, has to say on the subject. She presents the case of a man (she calls him "you") who is on the executive end of an enterprise and feels he should be on the planning end. "In that case," she writes, "your problem is to bring your talents to the attention of your superior officers with as little crowding and bustling as possible. Learn to write clear, short, definite memoranda and present them to your immediate superior until you are perfectly certain that he will never act upon them. In no other circumstances are you justified in going over his head." Very well, let us start from Mrs. Brande's so-called point of justification in going over your superior's head, and see what happens.

Let us suppose that you have presented your favorite memoranda to your immediate superior, Mr. Sutphen, twice and nothing has happened. You are still not perfectly certain that

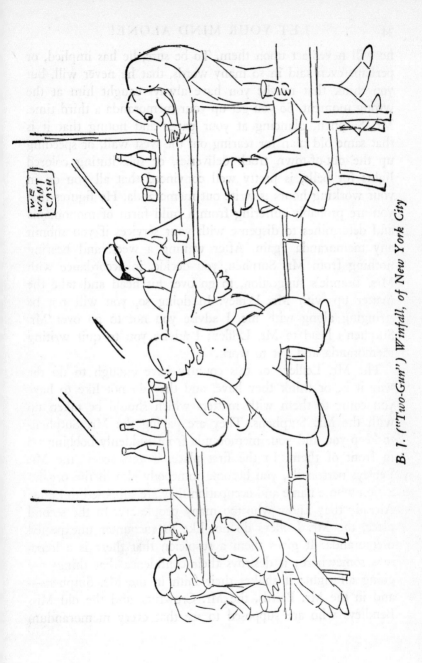

B. I. ("Two-Gun") Winfall, of New York City

he will never act upon them. To be sure, he has implied, or perhaps even said in so many words, that he never will, but you think that maybe you have always caught him at the wrong moment. So you get up your memoranda a third time. Mr. Sutphen, glancing at your paper and noting that it is that same old plan for tearing out the west wall, or speeding up the out-of-town truck deliveries, or substituting colored lights for bells, is pretty well convinced that all you do in your working hours is write out memoranda. He figures that you are probably suffering from a mild form of monomania and determines to dispense with your services if you submit any memoranda again. After waiting a week and hearing nothing from Mr. Sutphen, you decide, in accordance with Mrs. Brande's suggestion, to go over his head and take the matter up with Mr. Leffley. In doing so, you will not be stringing along with me. I advise you not to go over Mr. Sutphen's head to Mr. Leffley; I advise you to quit writing memoranda and get to work.

The Mr. Leffleys of this country have enough to do the way it is, or think they have, and they do not like to have you come to them with matters which should be taken up with the Mr. Sutphens. They are paying the Mr. Sutphens to keep you and your memoranda from suddenly bobbing up in front of them. In the first place, if you accost the Mr. Leffleys personally, you become somebody else in the organization whose name and occupation they are supposed to know. Already they know who too many people are. In the second place, the Mr. Leffleys do not like to encounter unexpected memoranda. It gives them a suspicion that there is a looseness somewhere; it destroys their confidence that things are going all right; it shakes their faith in the Mr. Sutphens—and in the Mr. Bairds, the Mr. Crowfuts, and the old Miss Bendleys who are supposed to see that every memorandum has been filed away, or is being acted on. I know of one young man who was always sending to his particular Mr. Leffley, over Mr. Sutphen's head, memoranda done up in limp-leather covers and tied with ribbon, this to show that he was not only clear, short, and definite, but neat. Mr. Leffley did not even glance between the leather covers; he simply told Miss Bendley to turn the thing over to Mr. Sutphen, who had already seen it. The young man was let go and is now a process-server. Keep, I say, your clear, short, and definite memoranda to yourself. If Mr. Sutphen has said no, he means no. If he has taken no action, no action is going to be taken. People who are all the time submitting memoranda are put down as jealous, disgruntled, and vaguely dangerous. Employers do not want them around. Sooner or later Mr. Sutphen, or Mr. Leffley himself, sees to it that a printed slip, clear, short, and definite, is put in their pay envelopes.

My own experience, and the experience of many of my friends, in dealing with superiors has covered a wide range of crucial situations of which these success writers appear to be oblivious and for which they therefore have no recommended course of action (which is probably just as well). I am reminded of the case of Mr. Russell Soames, a friend of mine, who worked for a man whom we shall call Mr. B. J. Winfall. This Winfall, some five or six years ago, in the days when Capone was at large and wholesale shootings were common in Chicago, called Soames into his office and said, "Soames, I'm going out to Chicago on that Weltmer deal and I want you to go along with me." "All right, Mr. Winfall," said Soames. They went to Chicago and had been there only four or five hours when they were calling each other Russell and B. J. and fighting for the check at the bar. On the third day, B. J. called Russell into his bedroom (B. J. had not left his bedroom in thirty-six hours) and said, "Russell, before we go back to New York, I want to see a dive, a hideout, a joint. I want to see these gangsters in their haunts. I want to see them in action, by God, if they ever get into action. I think most of it is newspaper talk. Your average gangster is a yellow cur." B. J. poured himself another drink from a bottle on his bedside table and repeated, "A yellow cur." Drink, as you see, made B. J. pugnacious (he had already gone through his amorous phase). Russell Soames tried to argue his chief out of this perilous plan, but failed. When Russell would not contact the right parties to arrange for B. J.'s little expedition, B. J. contacted them himself, and finally got hold of a men who knew a man who could get them into a regular hangout of gorillas and finger men.

Along about midnight of the fourth day in Chicago, B. J. Winfall was ready to set out for the dive. He wore a cap, which covered his bald spot, and he had somehow got hold of a cheap, ill-fitting suit, an ensemble which he was pleased to believe gave him the effect of a hardboiled fellow; as a matter of fact, his nose glasses, his pink jowls, and his paunch betrayed him instantly for what he was, a sedentary business-man. Soames strove to dissuade his boss, even in the taxi on their way to the tough spot, but Winfall pooh-poohed him. "Pooh pooh, Russell," he snarled out of the corner of his mouth, unfamiliarly. "These kind of men are rats." He had brought a flask with him and drank copiously from it. "Rats," he said, "of the first order. The first order, Russell, my boy." Soames kept repeating that he felt B. J. was underating the dangerousness of the Chicago gangster and begged him to be on his good behavior when they got to the joint, if only for the sake of B. J.'s wife and children and his (Russell's) old mother. He exacted a reluctant promise that B. J. would behave himself, but he was by no means easy in his mind when their taxi finally stopped in front of a low, dark building in a far, dark street. "Leave it to me, Russell, my boy," said B. J. as they got out of the cab. "Leave it to me." Their driver refused to wait, and Russell, who paid him off, was just in time to restrain his employer from beating on the door of the place with both fists. Russell himself knocked, timidly. A thin Italian with deadly eyes opened the door a few inches, Russell mentioned a name, falteringly, and the man admitted them.

As Russell described it to me later, it was a dingy, smoky place with a rough bar across the back attended by a liver-faced barman with a dirty rag thrown over one shoulder, and only one eye. Leaning on the bar and sitting at tables were a lot of small tough-faced men. They all looked up sullenly when Russell and B. J. walked in. Russell felt that there was a movement of hands in pockets. Smiling amiably, blinking nervously, Russell took his companion's arm, but the latter broke away, strode to the bar, and shouted for whiskey. The bartender fixed his one eye on B. J. with the glowering, steady gaze Jack Dempsey used to give his opponents in the ring. He took his time slamming glasses and a bottle down on the bar. B. J. filled a glass, tossed it off, turned heavily, and faced the roomful of men. "I'm Two-Gun Winfall from New York City!" he shouted. "Anybody *want* anything?"

By the most cringing, obsequious explanations and apologies, Russell Soames managed to get himself and his boss out of the place alive. The secret of accomplishing such a feat as he accomplished that night is not to be found in any of the inspirational books. Not a single one of their impressive bits of advice would get you anywhere. Take Mrs. Brande's now famous italicized exhortation, *"Act as if it were impossible to fail."* Wasn't B. J. Winfall doing exactly that? And was that any way to act in this particular situation? It was not. It was Russell Soames' craven apologies, his abject humility, his (as he told me later) tearful admission that he and B. J. were just drunken bums with broken hearts, that got them out of there alive. The success writers would never suggest, or even tolerate, any such behavior. If Russell Soames had followed their bright, hard rules of general conduct, he would be in his grave today and B. J. Winfall's wife would be a widow.

If Mrs. Brande is not, as in the case of the memoranda-writer, suggesting a relationship with a superior which I believe we have demonstrated to be dangerous and unworkable (and missing altogether the important problem of how to handle one's employer in his more difficult moments), she is dwelling mystically on the simple and realistic subject of how to deal with one's fellow-workers. Thus, in embroidering the theme that imagination can help you with your fellow-workers, she writes, "When you have seen this, you can work out a code for yourself which will remove many of the irritations and dissatisfactions of your daily work. Have you ever been amused and enlightened by seeing a familiar room from the top of the stepladder; or, in mirrors set at angles to each other, seen yourself as objectively for a second or two as anybody else in the room? It is that effect you should strive for in imagination." Here again I cannot hold with the dear lady. The nature of imagination, as she describes it, would merely terrify the average man. The idea of bringing such a distorted viewpoint of himself into his relation with his fellow-workers would twist his personality laboriously out of shape and, in the end, appall his fellow-workers. Men who catch an unfamiliar view of a room from the top of a stepladder are neither amused nor enlightened; they have a quick, gasping moment of vertigo which turns rapidly into plain terror. No man likes to see a familiar thing at an unfamiliar angle, or in an unfamiliar light, and this goes, above all things, for his own face. The glimpses that men get of themselves in mirrors set at angles to each other upset them for days. Frequently they shave in the dark for weeks thereafter. To ask a man to steadily contemplate this thing he has seen fleetingly in a mirror and to figure it as dealing with his fellow-workers day by day is to ask him to abandon his own character and to step into another, which he both disowns and dislikes. Split personality could easily result, leading to at least fifteen of the thirty-three "varieties of obliquity" which Mr. David Seabury lists in his "How to Worry Successfully," among them Cursory Enumeration, Distortion of Focus, Nervous Hesitation (superinduced by Ambivalence), Pseudo-Practicality, Divergency, Retardation, Emotionalized Compilation, Negative Dramatization, Rigidism, Secondary Adaptation, False Externalization, Non-Validation, Closure, and Circular Brooding.

I don't know why I am reminded at this point of my Aunt Kate Obetz, but I am. She was a woman without any imaginative la-di-da, without any working code save that of direct action, who ran a large dairy farm near Sugar Grove, Ohio, after her husband's death, and ran it successfully. One day something went wrong with the cream separator, and one of her hands came to her and said nobody on the farm could fix it. Should they send to town for a man? "No!" shouted my Aunt Kate. "I'll fix it myself!" Shouldering her way past a number of dairy workers, farm hands and members of her family, she grasped the cream separator and began monkeying with it. In a short time she had reduced it to even more pieces than it had been in when she took hold of it. She couldn't fix it. She was just making things worse. At length, she turned on the onlookers and bawled, "Why doesn't somebody take this goddam thing away from me?" Here was a woman as far out of the tradition of inspirationalist conduct as she could well be. She admitted failure; she had no code for removing irritations and dissatisfactions; she viewed herself as in a single mirror, directly; she lost her temper; she swore in the presence of subordinates; she confessed complete surrender in the face of a difficult problem; she didn't think of herself as a room seen from the top of a stepladder. And yet her workmen and her family continued to love and respect her. Somebody finally took the cream separator away from her; somehow it was fixed. Her failure did not show up in my aunt's character; she was always the same as ever.

For true guidance and sound advice in the business world we find, I think, that the success books are not the place to look, which is pretty much what I thought we would find all along.

6. Anodynes for Anxieties

I SHOULD LIKE TO BEGIN THIS LESSON WITH A QUOTATION FROM Mr. David Seabury's "How to Worry Successfully." When things get really tough for me, I always turn to this selection and read it through twice, the second time backward, and while it doesn't make me feel fine, exactly, it makes me feel better. Here it is:

"If you are indulging in gloomy fears which follow each other round and round until the brain reels, there are two possible procedures:

"First, quit circling. It doesn't matter where you cease whirling, as long as you stop.

"Second, if you cannot find a constant, think of something as different from the fact at which you stopped as you possibly can. Imagine what would happen if you mixed that contrast into your situation. If nothing results to clarify your worry, try another set of opposites and continue the process until you do get a helpful answer. If you persist, you will soon solve any ordinary problem."

I first read this remarkable piece of advice two months ago and I vaguely realized then that in it, somewhere, was a strangely familiar formula, not, to be sure, a formula that would ever help me solve anything, but a formula for something or other. And one day I hit on it. It is the formula by which the Marx brothers construct their dialogue. Let us take their justly famous scene in which Groucho says to Chico, "It is my belief that the missing picture is hidden in the house next door." Here Groucho has ceased whirling, or circling, and has stopped at a fact, that fact being his belief that the picture is hidden in the house next door. Now Chico, in accordance with Mr. Seabury's instructions, thinks of something as different from that fact as he possibly can. He says, "There isn't any house next door." Thereupon Groucho "mixes that contrast into his situation." He says, "Then we'll build one!"

The Filing-card System

Mr. Seabury says, "If you persist you will soon solve any ordinary problem." He underestimates the power of his formula. If you persist, you will soon solve anything at all, no matter how impossible. That way, of course, lies madness, but I would be the last person to say that madness is not a solution.

It will come as no surprise to you, I am sure, that throughout the Mentality Books with which we have been concerned there runs a thin, wavy line of this particular kind of Marxist philosophy. Mr. Seabury's works are heavily threaded with it, but before we continue with him, let us turn for a moment to dear Dorothea Brande, whose "Wake Up and Live!" has changed the lives of God knows how many people by this time. Writes Mrs. Brande, "One of the most famous men in America constantly sends himself postcards, and occasionally notes. He explained the card sending as being his way of relieving his memory of unnecessary details. In his pocket he carries a few postals addressed to his office. I was with him one threatening day when he looked out the restaurant window, drew a card from his pocket, and wrote on it. Then he threw it across the table to me with a grin. It was addressed to himself at his office, and said. 'Put your raincoat with your hat.' At the office he had other cards addressed to himself at home."

We have here a muzziness of thought so enormous that it is difficult to analyze. First of all, however, the ordinary mind is struck by the obvious fact that the famous American in question has, to relieve his memory of unnecessary details, burdened that memory with the details of having to have postcards at his office, in his pockets, and at his home all the time. If it isn't harder to remember always to take self-addressed postcards with you wherever you go than to remember to put your raincoat with your hat when the weather looks threatening, then you and I will eat the postcards or even the raincoat. Threatening weather itself is a natural sharp reminder of one's raincoat, but what is there to remind one that one is running out of postcards? And supposing the famous man does run out of postcards, what does he do—hunt up a Western Union and send himself a telegram? You can see how monstrously wrapped up in the coils of his own little memory system this notable American must soon find himself. There is something about this system of buying postcards, addressing them to oneself, writing messages on them, and then mailing them that is not unlike one of those elaborate Rube Goldberg contraptions taking up a whole room and involving bicycles, shotguns, parrots, and little colored boys, all set up for the purpose of eliminating the bother of, let us say, setting an alarm clock. Somehow, I can just see Mrs. Brande's famous man at his desk. On it there are two phones, one in the Bryant exchange, the other in the Vanderbilt exchange. When he wants to remind himself of something frightfully urgent, he picks up the Bryant phone and calls the Vanderbilt number, and when that phone rings, he picks it up and says hello and then carries on a conversation with himself. "Remember tomorrow is wifey's birthday!" he shouts over one phone. "O.K.!" he bawls back into the other. This, it seems to me, is a fair enough extension of the activities of our famous gentleman. There is no doubt, either, but that the two-phone system would make the date stick more sharply in his mind than if he just wrote it down on a memo pad. But to intimate that all this shows a rational disciplining of the mind, a development of the power of the human intellect, an approach to the Masterful Adjustment of which our Success Writers are so enamored, is to intimate that when Groucho gets the house built next door, the missing picture will be found in it.

When it comes to anxieties and worries, Mr. Seabury's elaborate systems for their relief or solution make the device of Mrs. Brande's famous American look childishly simple. Mr. Seabury knows, and apparently approves of, a man "who assists himself by fancied interviews with wise advisers. If he is in money difficulties, he has mental conversations with a banker; when business problems press, he seeks the aid of a great industrialist and talks his problems over with this ghostly friend until he comes to a definite conclusion." Here, unless I am greatly mistaken, we have wish fulfillment, fantasy, reverie, and woolgathering at their most perilous. This kind of goings-on with a ghostly banker or industrialist is an escape mechanism calculated to take a man so far from reality he might never get back. I tried it out myself one night just before Christmas when I had got down to $60 in the bank and hadn't bought half my presents yet. I went to bed early that night and had Mr. J. P. Morgan call on me. I didn't have to go to his office; he heard I was in some difficulty and called on me, dropping everything else. He came right into my bedroom and sat on the edge of the bed. "Well, well, well," he said, "what's this I hear about you being down?" "I'm not so good, J. P.," I said, smiling wanly. "We'll have the roses back in those cheeks in no time," he said. "I'm not really sick," I told him. "I just need money." "Well, well, well," he exclaimed, heartily, "is *that* all we need?" "Yes, sir," I said. He took out a checkbook. "How'd a hundred thousand dollars do?" he asked, jovially. "That would be all right," I said. "Could you give it to me in cash, though—in tens and twenties?" "Why, certainly, my boy, certainly," said Mr. Morgan, and he gave me the money in tens and twenties. "Thank you very much, J. P.," I said. "Not at all, Jim, not at all!" cried my ghostly friend. "What's going on in there?" shouted my wife, who was in the next room. It seems that I had got to talking out loud, first in my own voice and then louder, and with more authority, in Mr. Morgan's. "Nothing, darling," I answered. "Well, cut it out," she said. The depression that settled over me when I realized that I was just where I had been when I started to talk with Mr. Morgan was frightful. I haven't got completely over it yet.

This mental-conversation business is nothing, however, compared to what Mr. Seabury calls "picture-puzzle making in worry." To employ this aid in successful thinking, you have to have fifty or sixty filing cards, or blank cards of some kind or other. To show you how it works, let us follow the case history of one Frank Fordson as Mr. Seabury relates it. It seems that this Fordson, out of work, is walking the streets. "He enters store after store with discouraged, pessimistic proprietors. There are poor show windows and dusty sidewalks. They make Frank morbid. His mind feels heavy. He wishes he could happen on a bright idea." He does, as you shall see. Frank consults a psychologist. This psychologist tells him to take fifty filing cards and write on each of them a fact connected with his being out of work. So he writes on one "out of work" and on another "dusty sidewalks" and on another "poor show windows," etc. You and I would not be able to write down more than fifteen things like that before getting off onto something else, like "I hate Joe Grubig" or "Now is the time for all good men," but Frank can do fifty in his stride, all about how tough things are. This would so depress the ordinary mind that it would go home to bed, but not Frank. Frank puts all of the fifty cards on the floor of the psychologist's office and begins to couple them up at random, finally bringing into accidental juxtaposition the one saying "out of work" and one saying "dull sign." Well, out of this haphazard arrangement of the cards, Frank, Mr. Seabury says, got an idea. He went to a hardware store the next day and offered to shine the store's dull sign if the proprietor would give him a can of polish and let him keep what was left. Then he went around shining other signs, for money, and made $3 that day. Ten days later he got a job as a window-dresser and, before the year was out, a "position in advertising."

"Take one of your own anxieties," writes Mr. Seabury. "Analyze it so as to recall all the factors. Write three score of these on separate cards. Move the cards about on the floor into as many different relations as possible. Study each combination." Mr. Seabury may not know it, but the possible different relations of sixty cards would run into the millions.

If a man actually studied each of these combinations, it would at least keep him off the streets and out of trouble—and also out of the advertising business, which would be something, after all. Toy soldiers, however, are more fun.

Now, if this kind of playing with filing cards doesn't strike your fancy, there is the "Worry Play." Let me quote Mr. Seabury again. "You should write out a description of your worry," he says, "divide it into three acts and nine scenes, as if it were a play, and imagine it on the stage, or in the movies, with various endings. Look at it as impersonally as you would look at a comedy and you might be surprised at the detachment you would gain." I have tried very hard to do this. I try out all these suggestions. They have taken up most of my time and energy for the past six months and got me into such a state that my doctor says I can do only three more of these articles at the outside before I go to a sanitarium. A few years ago I had an old anxiety and I was reminded of it by this "Worry Play" idea. Although this old anxiety has been dead and gone for a long time, it kept popping up in my mind because, of all the worries I ever had, it seemed to lend itself best to the drama. I tried not to think about it, but there it was, and I finally realized I would have to write it out and imagine it on the stage before I could dismiss it from my consciousness and get back to work. Well, it ran almost as long as "Mourning Becomes Electra" and took me a little over three weeks to dramatize. Then, when I thought I was rid of it, I dreamed one night I had sold the movie rights, and so I had to adapt it to the movies (a Mr. Sam Maschino, a movie agent, kept bobbing up in my dreams, hectoring me). This took another two weeks. I could not, however, attain this detachment that Mr. Seabury talks about. Since the old anxiety was my own anxiety, I was the main character in it. Sometimes, for as many as fifteen pages of the play script and the movie continuity, I was the only person on the set. I visualized myself in the main rôle, naturally—having rejected Leslie Howard, John Gielgud, and Lionel Barrymore for one reason or another. I was lousy in the part, too, and that worried me. Hence I advise you not to write out your worries in the form of a play. It is simpler to write them out on sixty pieces of paper and juggle them around. Or talk about them to J. P. Morgan. Or send postcards to yourself about them. There are a number of solutions for anxieties which I believe are better than any of these, however: go out and skate, or take in a basketball game, or call on a girl. Or burn up a lot of books.

7. The Conscious vs. The Unconscious

IT IS HIGH TIME THAT WE WERE GETTING AROUND TO A CONSIDERATION of the magnum opus of Louis E. Bisch, M.D., Ph.D., formerly Professor of Neuropsychiatry at the New York Polyclinic Medical School and Hospital, and Associate in Educational Psychology at Columbia University, and the author of "Be Glad You're Neurotic." Some of the reassuring chapter titles of his popular treatise are "I'm a Neurotic Myself and Delighted," "You Hate Yourself. No Wonder!," "No, You're Not Going Insane Nor Will Any of Your Fears Come True," "Are Your Glands on Friendly Terms?," and "Of Course Your Sex Life Is Far from Satisfactory." Some of you will be satisfied with just these titles and will not go on to the book itself, on the ground that you have a pretty good idea of it already. I should like, however, to have you turn with me to Chapter VII, one of my favorite chapters in all psychomentology, "Your Errors and Compulsions Are Calls for Help."

The point of this chapter, briefly, is that the unconscious mind often opposes what the conscious mind wants to do or say, and frequently trips it up with all kinds of evasions, deceits, gags, and kicks in the pants. Our popular psychiatrists try to make these mysteries clear to the layman by the use of simple, homely language, and I am trying to do the same.

Dr. Bisch relates a lot of conflicts and struggles that take place between the Hercules of the Conscious and the Augean Stables of the Unconscious (that is my own colorful, if somewhat labored, metaphor and I don't want to see any of the other boys swiping it). "I myself," writes Dr. Bisch, "forgot the number of a hospital where I was to deliver a lecture when

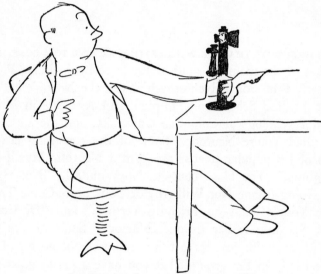

Psychiatrist about to Phone His Wife

I was about to apologize for my delay. I had talked to that particular hospital perhaps a hundred times before. This was the first time, however, that I was consciously trying to do what unconsciously I did not want to do." If you want unconsciously as well as consciously to call a hospital one hundred times out of one hundred and one, I say your conscious and unconscious are on pretty friendly terms. I say you are doing fine. This little experience of Dr. Bisch's is merely to give you a general idea of the nature of the chapter and to ease you into the discussion gently. There are many more interesting examples of conflict and error, of compulsion and obsession, to come. "A colleague," goes on Dr. Bisch, "told me that when he decided to telephone his wife to say he could not be home for dinner he dialled three wrong numbers before he got his own. 'It's because she always flares up when I'm detained at the office,' he explained." This shows that psychiatrists are just as scared of their wives as anybody else. Of course, I believe that this particular psychiatrist dialled the three wrong numbers on purpose. In the case of all husbands, both neurotic and normal, this is known as sparring for time and has no real psychological significance.

I almost never, I find in going slowly and carefully through Dr. Bisch's chapter, taking case histories in their order, agree with him. He writes, "The appearance of persons whom one dislikes or is jealous of, who have offended in some way or whom one fears, tend to be blotted from the mind." Well, some twelve years ago I knew, disliked, was jealous of, feared, and had been offended by a man whom I shall call Philip Vause. His appearance has not only not been blotted from my mind, it hasn't even tended to be. I can call it up as perfectly as if I were holding a photograph of the man in my hand. In nightmares I still dream of Philip Vause. When, in these dreams, I get on subways, he is the guard; when I fly through the air, the eagle that races with me has his face; when I climb the Eiffel Tower, there he is at the top, his black hair roached back, the mole on the left cheek, the thin-lipped smile, and all. Dr. Bisch goes on to say that "the more disagreeable an incident, the deeper is it finally repressed." To which he adds, "The recollection of the pain attending child-birth never lingers long." He has me there.

Dr. Bisch proceeds from that into this: "A man who mislays

his hat either dislikes it, wants a new one, experienced unpleasantness when last he wore it, or he does not want to go out. And what you lose you may be sure you do not value, even if it be your wedding ring. Psychologists claim that we lose things because we want to be rid of them or the association they carry, but that we are unwilling to admit the fact to ourselves and actually throw the thing away." This shows you pretty clearly, I think, the point psychologists have reached. I call it mysticism, but I am a polite fellow; you can call it anything you want to. Under any name, it isn't getting us anywhere. Every husband whose tearful wife has lost her wedding ring will now begin to brood, believing (if he strings along with the psychologists instead of with me) that the little darling threw it away, because she is really in love with Philip Vause, and that her tears over her loss are as phony as the plight of a panhandler's family. Let us leave all the sad young couples on the point of separating and go on to Dr. Bisch's analysis of a certain man.

"A certain man," writes Dr. Bisch, "forgot to wind the alarm on several occasions, in consequence of which he was late for work. He also forgot his keys on two occasions and had to wake up his wife in the early hours of the morning. Twice he forgot the furnace at night with the result that there was no heat the next day. In this case the unconscious was trying to tell him that he did not like living in the country although consciously he maintained that he did, for the good of the children." There are, from the standpoint of my own school of psychology, so many fallacies in this piece of analysis that I hardly know where to begin. But let us begin at the beginning, with the failure to wind the alarm clock. Now, a man who does not want to stay home winds the clock so that it will wake him and he can get the hell out and go to the office. There is surely nothing sounder than this. Hence the failure to wind the alarm clock shows that his unconscious was trying to tell him that he did not want to go to the office any more but wanted to stay at his house in the country all the time. The key-forgetting business I simply do not believe. A man who has had to rout out his wife once in the early hours of the morning is not going to forget his key a second time. This is known as Thurber's Empirical Law No. 1. If Dr. Bisch had lived in the country as long and as happily as I have, he would know this simple and unmystical fact: any man can forget to fix the clock and the furnace; especially the furnace, because the clock is usually right where it can be seen, whereas the furnace isn't. Some husbands "forget" to bank the furnace because they have kept hearing funny noises in the cellar all evening and are simply scared to go down there. Hundreds of simple little conscious motives enter into life, Dr. Bisch, hundreds of them.

"A woman," goes on Dr. Bisch, "who wished to consult an attorney about a divorce wrote to him: 'I have been married 22 years.' But the second 2 had evidently been added afterward, indicating that probably she was embarrassed to admit not being able to make a go of it after living with the man so long." How's that again, Doctor? I may be dumb, but I don't exactly catch all that. Couldn't the woman have really been married only 2 years, and couldn't she have added the second 2 indicating that probably she was embarrassed to admit that she was giving up trying to make a go of it after living with the man so *short* a time? Maybe we better just drop this one.

"A woman," continues Dr. Bisch (this is another woman), "who was talking to me about an intended trip to the lakes of northern Italy said: 'I don't wish to visit Lavonia Bay.' She, herself, was surprised, as no such place exists. Inasmuch as the trip was to be a honeymoon, it was 'love, honor, and obey' that really was bothering her." I take off my hat to the Doctor's astonishing powers of divination here, because I never would have figured it out. Now that he has given me the key, I get it, of course. "Love, honor, and obey," love-honor-obey, Lavonia Bay. I wonder if he knows the one about the woman who asked the librarian for a copy of "In a Garden." What she really wanted was "Enoch Arden." I like Lavonia Bay better, though, because it is psycho-neurotic, whereas there was nothing the matter with the other poor woman; she just thought that the name of the book was "In a Garden." Dr. Bisch might very likely see something more in this, but the way I've always heard it was that she just thought the name was "In a Garden."

"When a usually efficient secretary," writes Dr. Bisch, "makes errors in typing or shorthand, the excuse of fatigue or indisposition should be taken with a grain of salt. Resentment may have developed toward the employer or the work, or something may unconsciously be bothering her. Some years ago my own secretary often hit the *t* key by mistake. I discovered a young man by the name of Thomas was courting her." That doesn't explain the mistakes of a secretary I had five or six years ago. I had never had a secretary before, and had, indeed, never dictated a letter up to that time. We got some strange results. One of these, in a letter to a man I hoped I would never hear from again, was this sentence: "I feel that the cuneo has, at any rate, garbled the deig." This was not owing to fatigue or indisposition, or to resentment, although there *was* a certain resentment—or even to a young man named Cuneo or Deig. It was simply owing to the fact that my secretary, an Eastern girl, could only understand part of what I, a Middle-Westerner, was saying. In those days, I talked even more than I do now as if I had steel wool in my mouth, and the young lady just did not "get" me. Being afraid to keep asking me what I was trying to say, she simply put down what it sounded like. I signed this particular letter, by the way, just as she wrote it, and I never heard again from the man I sent it to, which is what I had hoped would happen. Psychiatrists would contend that I talked unintelligibly because of that very hope, but this is because they don't know that in Ohio, to give just one example, the word "officials" is pronounced "fishuls," no matter what anybody hopes.

We now go on to the case of a gentleman who deviated from the normal, or uninteresting. "In dressing for a formal dinner," says Dr. Bisch, "a man put on a bright red bow tie. His enthusiasm was self-evident." That is all our psychiatrist says about this one, and I think he is letting it go much too easily; I sense a definite drop here. If I were to say to you that in dressing for a formal dinner last night I put on a bright red bow tie and you were to say merely, "Your enthusiasm was self-evident," I would give you a nasty look and go on to somebody else who would get a laugh out of it, or at least ask what the hell was the idea. For the purpose of analysis in this particular case, I think you would have to know who the man was, anyway. If it was Ernest Boyd, that's one thing; if it was Jack Dempsey, that's another thing; if it was Harpo Marx or Dave Chasen, that's still another thing, or two other things. I think you really have to know who the man was. If the idea was to get a laugh, I don't think it was so very good. As for Dr. Bisch's notion that the man was enthusiastic, I don't see that at all. I just don't see it. Enthusiastic about what?

Our psychiatrist, in this meaty chapter, takes up a great many more cases, many more than I can disagree with in the space at my disposal, but I can't very well leave out the one about the man and the potatoes, because it is one of my favorites. It seems that there kept running through this unfortunate gentleman's mind the words "mashed potatoes, boiled potatoes, mashed potatoes, boiled potatoes"—*that* old line.

This went on for days, and the poor fellow, who had a lot of other things he wanted to keep repeating, could only keep repeating that. "Here," says Dr. Bisch, "the difficulty lay in the fact that the man had previously received a reprimand from his employer regarding his easy-going ways with the men who were under him in his department. 'Don't be too soft!' the employer had shouted. 'Be hard!' That very evening his wife served French fried potatoes that were burnt. 'I should be hard with her, too,' he mused. The next day the 'mashed potatoes, boiled potatoes' had been born." Now my own analysis is that the fellow really wanted to kill (mash) his wife and then go out and get fried or boiled. My theory brings in the fried potatoes and Dr. Bisch's doesn't, or not so well, anyway. I might say, in conclusion, that I don't like fellows who muse about getting hard with their wives and then take it out in repeating some silly line over and over. If I were a psychiatrist, I would not bother with them. There are so many really important ailments to attend to.

8. Sex ex Machina

WITH THE DISAPPEARANCE OF THE GAS MANTLE AND THE advent of the short circuit, man's tranquillity began to be threatened by everything he put his hand on. Many people believe that it was a sad day indeed when Benjamin Franklin tied that key to a kite string and flew the kite in a thunderstorm; other people believe that if it hadn't been Franklin, it would have been someone else. As, of course, it was in the case of the harnessing of steam and the invention of the gas engine. At any rate, it has come about that so-called civilized man finds himself today surrounded by the myriad mechanical devices of a technological world. Writers of books on how to control your nerves, how to conquer fear, how to cultivate calm, how to be happy in spite of everything, are of several minds as regards the relation of man and the machine. Some of them are prone to believe that the mind and body, if properly disciplined, can get the upper hand of this mechanized existence. Others merely ignore the situation and go on to the profitable writing of more facile chapters of inspiration. Still others attribute the whole menace of the machine to sex, and so confuse the average reader that he cannot always be certain whether he has been knocked down by an automobile or is merely in love.

Dr. Bisch, the Be-Glad-You're-Neurotic man, has a remarkable chapter which deals, in part, with man, sex, and the machine. He examines the case of three hypothetical men who start across a street on a red light and get in the way of an oncoming automobile. A dodges successfully; B stands still, "accepting the situation with calm and resignation," thus becoming one of my favorite heroes in modern belles-lettres; and C hesitates, wavers, jumps backward and forward, and finally runs head on into the car. To lead you through Dr. Bisch's complete analysis of what was wrong with B and C would occupy your whole day. He mentions what the McDougallians would say ("Instinct!"), what the Freudians would retort ("Complexes!"), and what the behaviorists would shout ("Conditioned reflexes!"). He also brings in what the physiologists would say—deficient thyroid, hypoadrenal functioning, and so on. The average sedentary man of our time who is at all suggestible must emerge from this chapter believing that his chances of surviving a combination of instinct, complexes, reflexes, glands, sex, and present-day traffic conditions are about equal to those of a one-legged blind man trying to get out of a labyrinth.

Let us single out what Dr. Bisch thinks the Freudians would say about poor Mr. C, who ran right into the car. He writes, " 'Sex hunger,' the Freudians would declare. 'Always keyed up and irritable because of it. Undoubtedly suffers from insomnia and when he does sleep his dream life must be productive, distorted, and possibly frightening. Automobile unquestionably has sex significance for him . . . to C the car is both enticing and menacing at one and the same time. . . . A thorough analysis is indicated. . . . It might take months. But then, the man needs an analysis as much as food. He is heading for a complete nervous collapse.' " It is my studied opinion, not to put too fine a point on it, that Mr. C is heading for a good mangling, and that if he gets away with only a nervous collapse, it will be a miracle.

I have not always, I am sorry to say, been able to go the whole way with the Freudians, or even a very considerable distance. Even though, as Dr. Bisch says, "One must admit that the Freudians have had the best of it thus far. At least they have received the most publicity." It is in matters like their analysis of men and machines, of Mr. C and the automobile, that the Freudians and I part company. Of course, the analysis above is simply Dr. Bisch's idea of what the Freudians would say, but I think he has got it down pretty well. Dr. Bisch himself leans toward the Freudian analysis of Mr. C, for he says in this same chapter, "An automobile bearing down upon you may be a sex symbol at that, you know, especially if you dream it." It is my contention, of course, that even if you dream it, it is probably not a sex symbol, but merely an automobile bearing down upon you. And if it bears down upon you in real life, I am sure it is an automobile. I have seen the same behavior that characterized Mr. C displayed by a squirrel (Mr. S) that lives in the grounds of my house in the country. He is a fairly tame squirrel, happily mated and not sex-hungry, if I am any judge, but nevertheless he frequently runs out toward my automobile when I start down the driveway, and then hesitates, wavers, jumps forward and backward, and occasionally would run right into the car except that he is awfully fast on his feet and that I always hurriedly put on the brakes of the 1935 V-8 Sex Symbol that I drive.

I have seen this same behavior in the case of rabbits (notoriously uninfluenced by any sex symbols save those of other rabbits), dogs, pigeons, a doe, a young hawk (which flew at my car), a blue heron that I encountered on a country road in Vermont, and once, near Paul Smiths in the Adirondacks, a fox. They all acted exactly like Mr. C. The hawk, unhappily, was killed. All the others escaped with nothing worse, I suppose, than a complete nervous collapse. Although I cannot claim to have been conversant with the private life and the secret compulsions, the psychoneuroses and the glandular activities of all these animals, it is nevertheless my confident and unswervable belief that there was nothing at all the matter with any one of them. Like Mr. C, they suddenly saw a car swiftly bearing down upon them, got excited, and lost their heads. I do not believe, you see, there was anything the matter with Mr. C, either. But I do believe that, after a thorough analysis lasting months, with a lot of harping on the incident of the automobile, something might very well come to be the

Happily-mated Rabbit Terrified by Motor-car

matter with him. He might even actually get to suffering from the delusion that he believes automobiles are sex symbols.

It seems to me worthy of note that Dr. Bisch, in reciting the reactions of three persons in the face of an oncoming car, selected three men. What would have happened had they been Mrs. A, Mrs. B, and Mrs. C? You know as well as I do: all

three of them would have hesitated, wavered, jumped forward
and backward, and finally run head on into the car if some
man hadn't grabbed them. (I used to know a motorist who,
every time he approached a woman standing on a curb prepar-
ing to cross the street, shouted, "Hold it, stupid!") It is not too
much to say that, with a car bearing down upon them, ninety-
five women out of a hundred would act like Mr. C—or Mr.
S, the squirrel, or Mr. F, the fox. But it is certainly too much
to say that ninety-five out of every hundred women look upon
an automobile as a sex symbol. For one thing, Dr. Bisch
points out that the automobile serves as a sex symbol because
of the "mechanical principle involved." But only one woman
in a thousand really knows anything about the mechanical
principle involved in an automobile. And yet, as I have said,
ninety-five out of a hundred would hesitate, waver, and jump,
just as Mr. C did. I think we have the Freudians here. If we
haven't proved our case with rabbits and a blue heron, we
have certainly proved it with women.

To my notion, the effect of the automobile and of other
mechanical contrivances on the state of our nerves, minds, and
spirits is a problem which the popular psychologists whom I
have dealt with know very little about. The sexual explanation of the relationship of man and the machine is not good
enough. To arrive at the real explanation, we have to begin
very far back, as far back as Franklin and the kite, or at least as
far back as a certain man and woman who appear in a book
of stories written more than sixty years ago by Max Adeler.
One story in this book tells about a housewife who bought
a combination ironing board and card table, which some
New England genius had thought up in his spare time. The
husband, coming home to find the devilish contraption in the
parlor, was appalled. "What is that thing?" he demanded. His
wife explained that it was a card table, but that if you pressed

a button underneath, it would become an ironing board. Whereupon she pushed the button and the table leaped a foot into the air, extended itself, and became an ironing board. The story goes on to tell how the thing finally became so finely sensitized that it would change back and forth if you merely touched it—you didn't have to push the button. The husband stuck it in the attic (after it had leaped up and struck him a couple of times while he was playing euchre), and on windy nights it could be heard flopping and banging around, changing from a card table to an ironing board and back. The story serves as one example of our dread heritage of annoyance, shock, and terror arising out of the nature of mechanical contrivances *per se*. The mechanical principle involved in this damnable invention had, I believe, no relationship to sex whatsoever. There are certain analysts who see sex in anything, even a leaping ironing board, but I think we can ignore these scientists.

No man (to go on) who has wrestled with a self-adjusting card table can ever be quite the man he once was. If he arrives at the state where he hesitates, wavers, and jumps at every mechanical device he encounters, it is not, I submit, because he recognizes the enticements of sex in the device, but only because he recognizes the menace of the machine as such. There might very well be, in every descendant of the man we have been discussing, an inherited desire to jump at, and conquer, mechanical devices before they have a chance to turn into something twice as big and twice as menacing. It is not reasonable to expect that his children and their children will have entirely escaped the stigma of such traumata. I myself will never be the man I once was, nor will my descendants probably ever amount to much, because of a certain experience I had with an automobile.

I had gone out to the barn of my country place, a barn

which was used both as a garage and a kennel, to quiet some large black poodles. It was 1 A.M. of a pitch-dark night in winter and the poodles had apparently been terrified by some kind of a prowler, a tramp, a turtle, or perhaps a fiend of some sort. Both my poodles and I myself believed, at the time, in fiends, and still do. Fiends who materialize out of nothing and nowhere, like winged pigweed or Russian thistle. I had quite a time quieting the dogs, because their panic spread to me and mine spread back to them again, in a kind of vicious circle. Finally, a hush as ominous as their uproar fell upon them, but they kept looking over their shoulders, in a kind of apprehensive way. "There's nothing to be afraid of," I told them as firmly as I could, and just at that moment the klaxon of my car, which was just behind me, began to shriek. Everybody has heard a klaxon on a car suddenly begin to sound; I understand it is a short circuit that causes it. But very few people have heard one scream behind them while they were quieting six or eight alarmed poodles in the middle of the night in an old barn. I jump now whenever I hear a klaxon, even the klaxon on my own car when I push the button intentionally. The experience has left its mark. Everybody, from the day of the jumping card table to the day of the screaming klaxon, has had similar shocks. You can see the result, entirely unsuperinduced by sex, in the strained faces and muttering lips of people who pass you on the streets of great, highly mechanized cities. There goes a man who picked up one of those trick matchboxes that whir in your hands; there goes a woman who tried to change a fuse without turning off the current; and yonder toddles an ancient who cranked an old Reo with the spark advanced. Every person carries in his consciousness the old scar, or the fresh wound, of some harrowing misadventure with a contraption of some sort. I know people who would not deposit a nickel and a dime in a cigarette-vending machine and push the lever even if a diamond necklace came out. I know dozens who would not climb into an airplane even if it didn't move off the ground. In none of these people have I discerned what I would call a neurosis, an "exaggerated" fear; I have discerned only a natural caution in a world made up of gadgets that whir and whine and whiz and shriek and sometimes explode.

I should like to end with the case history of a friend of mine in Ohio named Harvey Lake. When he was only nineteen, the steering bar of an old electric runabout broke off in his hand, causing the machine to carry him through a fence and into the grounds of the Columbus School for Girls. He developed a fear of automobiles, trains, and every other kind of vehicle that was not pulled by a horse. Now, the psychologists would call this a complex and represent the fear as abnormal, but I see it as a purely reasonable apprehension. If Harvey Lake had, because he was catapulted into the grounds of the Columbus School for Girls, developed a fear of girls, I would call that a complex; but I don't call his normal fear of machines a complex. Harvey Lake never in his life got into a plane (he died in a fall from a porch), but I do not regard that as neurotic, either, but only sensible.

I have, to be sure, encountered men with complexes. There was, for example, Marvin Belt. He had a complex about airplanes that was quite interesting. He was not afraid of machinery, or of high places, or of crashes. He was simply afraid that the pilot of any plane he got into might lose his mind. "I imagine myself high over Montana," he once said to me, "in a huge, perfectly safe tri-motored plane. Several of the passengers are dozing, others are reading, but I am keeping my eyes glued on the door to the cockpit. Suddenly the pilot steps out of it, a wild light in his eyes, and in a falsetto like that of a little girl he says to me, 'Conductor, will you please let me off at One-Hundred-and-Twenty-fifth Street?' " "But," I said to Belt, "even if the pilot does go crazy, there is still the co-pilot." "No, there isn't," said Belt. "The pilot has hit the co-pilot over the head with something and killed him." Yes, the psychoanalysts can have Marvin Belt. But they can't have Harvey Lake, or Mr. C, or Mr. S, or Mr. F, or, while I have my strength, me.

9. Sample Intelligence Test

THE FUZZINESS THAT CREEPS INTO THE THOUGHT PROCESSES of those inspirationalists who seek to clarify the human scene reaches an interesting point in Chapter XIV of "How to Develop Your Personality," by Sadie Myers Shellow, Ph.D. Dr. Shellow was formerly psychologist with the Milwaukee Electric Railway & Light Company. These things happen in a world of endless permutations. I myself was once connected with the Central Ohio Optical Company. I was hired because I had a bicycle, although why an optical company would want a bicycle might appear on the face of it as inexplicable as why a railway-and-light company would want a psychologist. My experience of motormen leads me to believe that they are inarticulate to the point of never saying anything at all, and I doubt if there is a motorman in all Wisconsin who would reveal the story of his early childhood to a psychologist. Dr. Shellow, of course, may have proceeded along some other line, but most psychologists start with your childhood. Or with your sex life. I somehow have never thought of motormen as having sex lives, but this doesn't mean that they don't have them. I feel that this speculation is not getting us anywhere.

Let us return to Dr. Shellow's book. It was first published five years ago, but her publishers have just brought out a dollar edition, which puts the confusion in Chapter XIV within reach of everyone. In 1932, the book went into six printings. The present edition was printed from the original plates, which means that the mistakes which appear in it have gone on and

Motorman Concealing His Sex Life from a Woman Psychologist

on through the years. The book begins with a prefatory note by Albert Edward Wiggam, a foreword by Morris S. Viteles, and an introduction by Dr. Shellow herself. In Chapter I, first paragraph, Dr. Shellow gives the dictionary definition of "personality" as follows: "The sum total of traits necessary to describe what is to be a person." Unless I have gone crazy reading all these books, and I think I have, that sentence defines personality as the sum total of traits necessary to describe an unborn child. If Dr. Shellow's error here is typographical, it looms especially large in a book containing a chapter that tells how to acquire reading skill and gives tests for efficiency in reading. Dr. Shellow tells of a young woman who "was able to take in a whole page at a glance, and through concentrated attention relate in detail what she had read as the words flashed by." If Dr. Shellow used this system in reading the proofs of her book, the system is apparently no good. It certainly *sounds* as if it were no good. I have started out with an admittedly minor confusion—the definition of personality —but let us go on to something so mixed up that it becomes almost magnificent.

Chapter XIV is called "Intelligence Tests," and under the heading "Sample Intelligence Test" twelve problems are posed. There are some pretty fuzzy goings-on in the explanation of No. 11, but it is No. 12 that interests me most; what the Milwaukee motormen made of it I can't imagine. No. 12 is stated as follows: "Cross out the *one* word which makes this sentence absurd and substitute one that is correct: A pound of feathers is lighter than a pound of lead." Let us now proceed to Dr. Shellow's explanation of how to arrive at the solution of this toughy. She writes, "In 12 we get at the critical ability of the mind. Our first impulse is to agree that a pound of feathers is lighter than a pound of lead, since feathers are lighter than lead, but if we look back, we will see that a *pound* of feathers could be no lighter than a *pound* of lead since a pound is always the same. What one word, then, makes the whole sentence absurd? We might cross out the second pound and substitute ounce, in which case we would have: A pound of feathers is heavier than an ounce of lead, and that would be correct. Or we might cross out the word heavier and substitute bulkier, in which case we would have eliminated the absurdity."

We have here what I can only call a paradise of errors. I find, in Dr. Shellow's presentation of the problem and her solution of it, Transference, Wishful Thinking, Unconscious Substitution, Psychological Dissociation, Gordian Knot Cutting, Cursory Enumeration, Distortion of Focus, Abandonment of Specific Gravity, Falsification of Premise, Divergence from Consistency, Overemphasis on Italics, Rhetorical Escapism, and Disregard of the Indefinite Article. Her major error—the conjuring up of the word "heavier" out of nowhere—is enough to gum up any problem beyond repair, but there are other interesting pieces of woolly reasoning in No. 12. Dr. Shellow gets off on the wrong foot in her very presentation of the problem. She begins, "Cross out the *one* word which makes this sentence absurd." That means there is *only* one word which can be changed and restricts the person taking the test to that one word, but Dr. Shellow goes on, in her explanation, to change first one and then another. As a matter of fact, there are five words in the sentence any one of which can be changed to give the sentence meaning. Thus we are all balled up at the start. If Dr. Shellow had written, "Cross out one word which makes this sentence absurd," that would have been all right. I think I know how she got into trouble. I imagine that she originally began, "Cross out one of the words," and found herself face to face with that ancient stumbling block in English composition, whether to say "which *makes* this sentence absurd" or "which *make* this sentence absurd." (I don't like to go into italics, but to straighten Dr. Shellow out you got to go into italics.) I have a notion that Dr. Shellow decided that "make" was right, which of course it is, but that she was dissatisfied with "Cross out one of the words which make this sentence absurd" because here "words" dominates "one." Since she wanted to emphasize "one," she italicized it and then, for good measure, put the definite article "the" in front of it. That would have given her "Cross out the *one* of the words which make this sentence absurd." From there she finally arrived at what she arrived at, and the problem began slowly to close in on her.

I wouldn't dwell on this at such length if Dr. Shellow's publishers had not set her up as a paragon of lucidity, precision, and logical thought. (Come to think that over, I believe I would dwell on it at the same length even if they hadn't.) Some poor fellows may have got inferiority complexes out of being unable to see through Dr. Shellow's authoritative explanation of No. 12, and I would like to restore their confidence in their own minds. You can't just go batting off any old sort of answer to an intelligence test in this day when every third person who reads these books has a pretty firm idea that his mind is cracking up.

Let us go on to another interesting fuzziness in the Doctor's explanation. Take her immortal sentence: "We might cross out the second pound and substitute ounce," etc. What anybody who followed those instructions would arrive at is: "A pound of feathers is lighter than *a* ounce of lead." Even leaving the matter of weight out of it (which I am reluctant to do, since weight is the main point), you can't substitute "ounce" for "pound" without substituting "an" for "a," thus changing two words. If "an" and "a" are the same word, then things have come to a pretty pass, indeed. If such slipshoddery were allowed, you could solve the problem with "A pound of feathers is lighter than two pound of lead." My own way out was to change "is" to "ain't," if anybody is interested.

Let us close this excursion into the wonderland of psychology with a paragraph of Dr. Shellow's which immediately follows her explanation of No. 12: "If the reader went through this test quickly before reading the explanation, he may have discovered some things about himself. A more detailed test would be even more revealing. Everyone should at some time or other take a good comprehensive intelligence test and analyze his own defects so that he may know into what errors his reasoning takes him and of what faulty habits of thought he must be aware." I want everybody to file out quietly, now, without any wisecracks.

10. Miscellaneous Mentation

IN GOING BACK OVER THE WELL-THUMBED PAGES OF MY LIBRARY of recent books on mental technique, I have come upon a number of provocative passages which I marked with a pencil but, for one reason or another, was unable to fit into any of my preceding chapters. I have decided to take up this group of miscellaneous matters here, treating the various passages in the order in which I come to them. First, then, there is a paragraph from Dr. Louis E. ("Be Glad You're Neurotic") Bisch, on Overcompensation. He writes, "To overcome a handicap and overcompensate is much the same as consciously and deliberately setting out to overcome a superstition. We will say that you are afraid to pass under a ladder. But suppose you defy the superstition and do it anyway? You may feel uneasy for a few hours or a few days. To your surprise, perhaps, nothing dreadful happens to you. This gives you courage. You try the ladder stunt again. Still you find yourself unharmed. After a while you look for ladders; you delight in walking under them; your ego has been pepped up and you defy all the demons that may be!"

Of course, the most obvious comment to be made here is that if you keep looking for and walking under ladders long enough, something *is* going to happen to you, in the very nature of things. Then, since your defiance of "all the demons that may be" proves you still believe in them, you will be right back where you were, afraid to walk under a ladder again. But what interests me most in Dr. Bisch's study of

Ladder Phobia

how to "pep up the ego" is its intensification of the very kind
of superstition which the person in this case sets out to defy
and destroy. To substitute walking under ladders for not walking under ladders is a distinction without a difference. For
here we have, in effect, a person who was afraid to walk under
ladders, and is now afraid not to. In the first place he avoided
ladders because he feared the very fear that that would put
into him. This the psychologists call phobophobia (they really
do). But *now* he is afraid of the very fear he had of being
afraid and hence is a victim of what I can only call pho-
bophobophobia, and is in even deeper than he was before. Let
us leave him in this perfectly frightful mess and turn to our
old authority, Mr. David Seabury, and a quite different kind of
problem.

"A young woman," writes Mr. Seabury, "remarked recently
that she had not continued her literary career because she
found her work commonplace. 'And,' she went on, 'I don't
want to fill the world with more mediocre writing.' 'What
sort of finished product do you expect a girl of twenty-two
to produce?' I asked. 'You are judging what you can be in the
future by what you are doing in the present. Would you
have a little elm tree a year old compare itself with a giant
tree and get an inferiority feeling? An elm tree of one year
is a measly little thing, but given time it shades a whole
house.'" Mr. Seabury does not take into consideration that,
given time, a lady writer shades a whole house, too, and that
whereas a little elm tree is bound to grow up to be a giant
elm tree, a lady writer who at twenty-two is commonplace
and mediocre is bound to grow to be a giant of common-
placeness and mediocrity. I think that this young woman is
the only young woman writer in the history of the United
States who thought that she ought not to go on with her
writing because it was mediocre. If ever a psychologist had it

in his power to pluck a brand from the burning, Mr. Seabury had it here. But what did he do? He made the young writer of commonplace things believe she would grow to be a veritable elm in the literary world. I hope she didn't listen to him, but I am afraid she probably did. Still, she sounds like a smart girl, and maybe she saw the weakness in Mr. Seabury's "You are judging what you can be in the future by what you are doing in the present." I can think of no sounder judgment to make.

Let us now look at something from Dr. James L. ("Streamline Your Mind") Mursell. In a chapter on "Mastering and Using Language," he brings out that most people do not know how to read. Dr. Mursell would have them get a precise and dogmatic meaning out of everything they read, thus leaving nothing to the fantasy and the imagination. This is particularly unfortunate, it seems to me, when applied to poetry, as Dr. Mursell applies it. He writes, "A large group of persons *seemed* to read the celebrated stanza beginning

> The Assyrian came down like the wolf on the fold
> And his cohorts were gleaming in purple and gold,

and ending

> Where the blue wave rolls nightly on deep Galilee.

"But when a suspicious-minded investigator tested them, quite a number turned out to suppose that the Assyrian's cohorts were an article of wearing apparel and that the last line referred to the astronomical discoveries of Galileo. Is this reading?"

Well, yes. What the second line means is simply that the *cohorts'* articles of wearing apparel were gleaming in purple and gold, so nothing much is distorted except the number of people who came down like the wolf on the fold. The readers who got it wrong had, it seems to me, as deep a poetic feeling (which is the main thing) as those who knew that a cohort was originally one of the ten divisions of a Roman legion and had, to begin with, three hundred soldiers, later five hundred to six hundred. Furthermore, those who got it wrong had a fine flaring image of one Assyrian coming down valiantly all alone, instead of with a couple of thousand soldiers to help him, the big coward. As for "Where the blue wave rolls nightly on deep Galilee," the reading into this of some vague association with the far, lonely figure of Galileo lends it a misty poetic enchantment which, to my way of thinking, the line can very well put up with. Dr. Mursell should be glad that some of the readers didn't think "the blue wave" meant the Yale football team. And even if they had, it would be all right with me. There is no person whose spirit hasn't at one time or another been enriched by some cherished transfiguring of meanings. Everybody is familiar with the youngster who thought the first line of the Lord's Prayer was "Our Father, who art in heaven, Halloween be thy Name." There must have been for him, in that reading, a thrill, a delight, and an exaltation that the exact sense of the line could not possibly have created. I once knew of a high-school teacher in a small town in Ohio who for years had read to his classes a line that actually went "She was playing coquette in the garden below" as if it were "She was playing croquet in the garden below." When, one day, a bright young scholar raised his hand and pointed out the mistake, the teacher said, grimly, "I have read that line my way for seventeen years and I intend to go on reading it my way." I am all for this point of view. I remember that, as a boy of eight, I thought "Post No Bills" meant that the walls on which it appeared belonged to one Post No Bill, a man of the same heroic proportions as Buffalo

Bill. Some suspicious-minded investigator cleared this up for me, and a part of the glamour of life was gone.

We will now look at a couple of items from the very latest big-selling inspirational volume, no less a volume than Mr. Dale Carnegie's "How to Win Friends and Influence People." Writes Mr. Carnegie, "The New York Telephone Company conducts a school to train its operators to say 'Number please' in a tone that means 'Good morning, I am happy to be of service to you.' Let's remember that when we answer the telephone tomorrow." Now it seems to me that if this is something we have deliberately to remember, some thing we have to be told about, then obviously the operators aren't getting their message over. And I don't think they are. What I have always detected in the voices of telephone operators is a note of peremptory willingness. Their tone always conveys to me "What number do you want? And don't mumble!" If it is true, however, that the operator's tone really means "Good morning, I am happy to be of service to you," then it is up to the subscriber to say, unless he is a curmudgeon, "Thank you. How are you this morning?" If Mr. Carnegie doesn't know what the operator would say to that, I can tell him. She would say, "I am sorry, sir, but we are not allowed to give out that information." And the subscriber and the operator would be right back where they are supposed to be, on a crisp, business-like basis, with no genuine "good morning" and no real happiness in it at all.

I also want to examine one of Mr. Carnegie's rules for behavior in a restaurant. He writes, "You don't have to wait until you are Ambassador to France or chairman of the Clambake Committee of the Elk's Club before you use this philosophy of appreciation. You can work magic with it every day. If, for example, the waitress brings us mashed potatoes when we ordered French fried, let's say 'I'm sorry to trouble you, but I prefer French fried.' She'll reply. 'No trouble at all,' and will be glad to do it because you have shown respect for her." Now, it is my belief that if we said to the waitress, "I'm sorry to trouble you, but I prefer French fried," she would say, "Well, make up ya mind." The thing to say to her is simply, "I asked for French fried potatoes, not mashed potatoes." To which, of course, she might reply, under her breath, "Well, take the marbles outa ya mouth when ya talkin'." There is no way to make a waitress really glad to do anything. Service is all a matter of business with her, as it is with the phone operators, and Mr. Carnegie might as well face the fact. Anyway, I do not see any "philosophy of appreciation" in saying to a waitress, "I'm sorry to trouble you, but I prefer French fried." Philosophy and appreciation are both capable of higher flights than that. "How are you, Beautiful?" is a higher form of appreciation than what Mr. Carnegie recommends, and it is not very high. But at least it isn't stuffy, and "I'm sorry to trouble you, but I prefer French fried" is; waitresses hate men who hand them that line.

For a final example of mistaken observation of life and analysis of people, I must turn again to the prolific Mr. Seabury. He writes that once, at a dinner, he sat opposite "a tall, lanky man with restless fingers" who was telling the lady on his right about his two dogs and their four puppies. "It was obvious," says Mr. Seabury, "that he had identified himself with the mother dog and was accustomed to spend a good deal of his time in conversation with her about the welfare of her young." Having been a dog man myself for a great many years, I feel that I am on sounder ground there than Mr. Seabury. I know that no dog man ever identifies himself with the mother dog. There is a type of dog man who sometimes wistfully identifies himself with the father dog, or would like to, at any rate, because of the comparative freedom, lack of responsibility, and general carefree attitude that marks the family life of all father dogs. But no dog man, as I have said, ever identifies himself with the mother dog. He may, to be sure, spend a good deal of his time in conversation with her, but this conversation is never about the welfare of her young. Every dog man knows that there is nothing he can say to any mother dog about the welfare of her young that will make the slightest impression on her. This is partly because she does not know enough English to carry on a conversation that would get very far, and partly because, even if she did, she would not let any suggestions or commands, coaxings or wheedlings, influence her in the least.

Every dog man, when his mother dog has had her first pups, has spent a long time fixing up a warm bed in a nice, airy corner for the mother dog to have her pups in, only to discover that she prefers to have them under the barn, in a hollow log, or in the dark and inaccessible reaches of a store-room amidst a lot of overshoes, ice skates, crokinole boards, and ball bats. Every dog man has, at the risk of his temper and his limbs, grimly and resolutely dug the mother dog and her pups out from among the litter of debris that she prefers, stepping on the ball bats, kneeling on the ice skates, and put her firmly into the bassinet he has prepared for her, only to have her carry the pups back to the nest among the overshoes and the crokinole boards during the night. In the end, every dog man has let the mother dog have her way, having discovered that there is nothing he can do, much less say, that will win her over to his viewpoint in the matter. She refuses to identify herself with him and he becomes too smart to try to identify himself with her. It would wear him to a frazzle in a week.

Part Two

Other More or Less Inspirational Pieces

1. The Breaking Up of the Winships

THE TROUBLE THAT BROKE UP THE GORDON WINSHIPS SEEMED to me, at first, as minor a problem as frost on a window-pane. Another day, a touch of sun, and it would be gone. I was inclined to laugh it off, and, indeed, as a friend of both Gordon and Marcia, I spent a great deal of time with each of them, separately, trying to get them to laugh it off, too—with him at his club, where he sat drinking Scotch and smoking too much, and with her in their apartment, that seemed so large and lonely without Gordon and his restless moving around and his quick laughter. But it was no good; they were both adamant. Their separation has lasted now more than six months. I doubt very much that they will ever go back together again.

It all started one night at Leonardo's, after dinner, over their Bénédictine. It started innocently enough, amiably even, with laughter from both of them, laughter that froze finally as the clock ran on and their words came out sharp and flat and stinging. They had been to see "Camille." Gordon hadn't liked it very much. Marcia had been crazy about it because she is crazy about Greta Garbo. She belongs to that consider-able army of Garbo admirers whose enchantment borders almost on fanaticism and sometimes even touches the edges of frenzy. I think that, before everything happened, Gordon

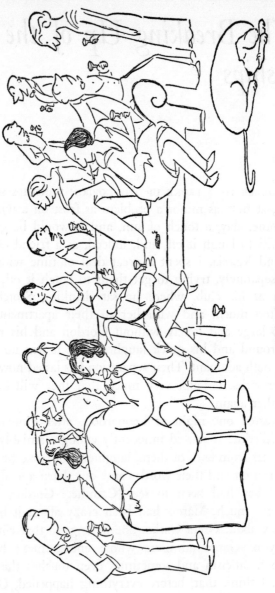

Cocktail Party, 1937

admired Garbo, too, but the depth of his wife's conviction that here was the greatest figure ever seen in our generation on sea or land, on screen or stage, exasperated him that night. Gordon hates (or used to) exaggeration, and he respects (or once did) detachment. It was his feeling that detachment is a necessary thread in the fabric of a woman's charm. He didn't like to see his wife get herself "into a sweat" over anything and, that night at Leonardo's, he unfortunately used that expression and made that accusation.

Marcia responded, as I get it, by saying, a little loudly (they had gone on to Scotch and soda), that a man who had no abandon of feeling and no passion for anything was not altogether a man, and that his so-called love of detachment simply covered up a lack of critical appreciation and understanding of the arts in general. Her sentences were becoming long and wavy, and her words formal. Gordon suddenly began to pooh-pooh her; he kept saying "Pooh!" (an annoying mannerism of his, I have always thought). He wouldn't answer her arguments or even listen to them. That, of course, infuriated her. "Oh, pooh to you, too!" she finally more or less shouted. He snapped at her, "Quiet, for God's sake! You're yelling like a prizefight manager!" Enraged at that, she had recourse to her eyes as weapons and looked steadily at him for a while with the expression of one who is viewing a small and horrible animal, such as a horned toad. They then sat in moody and brooding silence for a long time, without moving a muscle, at the end of which, getting a hold on herself, Marcia asked him, quietly enough, just exactly what actor on the screen or on the stage, living or dead, he considered greater than Garbo. Gordon thought a moment and then said, as quietly as she had put the question, "Donald Duck." I don't believe that he meant it at the time, or even thought that he meant it. However that may have been, she looked at him scornfully and said that that speech just about perfectly represented the shallowness of his intellect and the small range of his imagination. Gordon asked her not to make a spectacle of herself—she had raised her voice slightly—and went on to say that her failure to see the genius of Donald Duck proved conclusively to him that she was a woman without humor. That, he said, he had always suspected; now, he said, he knew it. She had a great desire to hit him, but instead she sat back and looked at him with her special Mona Lisa smile, a smile rather more of contempt than, as in the original, of mystery. Gordon hated that smile, so he said that Donald Duck happened to be exactly ten times as great as Garbo would ever be and that anybody with a brain in his head would admit it instantly. Thus the Winships went on and on, their resentment swelling, their sense of values blurring, until it ended up with her taking a taxi home alone (leaving her vanity bag and one glove behind her in the restaurant) and with him making the rounds of the late places and rolling up to his club around dawn. There, as he got out, he asked his taxi-driver which he liked better, Greta Garbo or Donald Duck, and the driver said he liked Greta Garbo best. Gordon said to him, bitterly, "Pooh to you, too, my good friend!" and went to bed.

The next day, as is usual with married couples, they were both contrite, but behind their contrition lay sleeping the ugly words each had used and the cold glances and the bitter gestures. She phoned him, because she was worried. She didn't want to be, but she was. When he hadn't come home, she was convinced he had gone to his club, but visions of him lying in a gutter or under a table, somehow horribly mangled, haunted her, and so at eight o'clock she called him up. Her heart lightened when he said, "Hullo," gruffly: he was alive, thank God! His heart may have lightened a little, too, but not very much, because he felt terrible. He felt terrible and he felt that it was her fault that he felt terrible. She said that she was sorry and that they had both been very silly, and he growled something about he was glad she realized *she'd* been silly, anyway. That attitude put a slight edge on the rest of her words. She asked him shortly if he was coming home. He said sure he was coming home; it was his home, wasn't it? She told him to go back to bed and not be such an old bear, and hung up.

The next incident occurred at the Clarkes' party a few days later. The Winships had arrived in fairly good spirits to find themselves in a buzzing group of cocktail-drinkers that more or less revolved around the tall and languid figure of the guest of honor, an eminent lady novelist. Gordon late in the evening won her attention and drew her apart for one drink together and, feeling a little high and happy at that time, as is the way with husbands, mentioned lightly enough (he wanted to get it out of his subconscious), the argument that he and his wife had had about the relative merits of Garbo and Duck. The tall lady, lowering her cigarette-holder, said, in the spirit of his own gaiety, that he could count her in on his side. Unfortunately, Marcia Winship, standing some ten feet away, talking to a man with a beard, caught not the spirit but only a few of the words of the conversation, and jumped to the conclusion that her husband was deliberately reopening the old wound, for the purpose of humiliating her in public. I think that in another moment Gordon might have brought her over, and put his arm around her, and admitted his "defeat" —he was feeling pretty fine. But when he caught her eye, she gazed through him, freezingly, and his heart went down. And then his anger rose.

Their fight, naturally enough, blazed out again in the taxi they took to go home from the party. Marcia wildly attacked the woman novelist (Marcia had had quite a few cocktails), defended Garbo, excoriated Gordon, and laid into Donald Duck. Gordon tried for a while to explain exactly what had happened, and then he met her resentment with a resentment that mounted even higher, the resentment of the misunderstood husband. In the midst of it all she slapped him. He looked at her for a second under lowered eyelids and then said, coldly, if a bit fuzzily, "This is the end, but I want you to go to your grave knowing that Donald Duck is *twenty times* the artist Garbo will ever be, the longest day you, or she, ever live, if you *do*—and I can't understand, with so little to live for, why you should!" Then he asked the driver to stop the car, and he got out, in wavering dignity. "Caricature! Cartoon!" she screamed after him. "You and Donald Duck both, you—" The driver drove on.

The last time I saw Gordon—he moved his things to the club the next day, forgetting the trousers to his evening clothes and his razor—he had convinced himself that the point at issue between him and Marcia was one of extreme importance involving both his honor and his integrity. He said that now it could never be wiped out and forgotten. He said that he sincerely believed Donald Duck was as great a creation as any animal in all the works of Lewis Carroll, probably even greater, perhaps much greater. He was drinking and there was a wild light in his eye. I reminded him of his old love of detachment, and he said to the hell with detachment. I laughed at him, but he wouldn't laugh. "If," he said, grimly, "Marcia persists in her silly belief that that Swede is great and that Donald Duck is merely a caricature, I cannot conscientiously live with her again. I believe that he is great, that the man who created him is a genius, probably our only genius. I believe, further, that Greta Garbo is just another actress. As God is my judge, I believe that! What does she expect me to do, go whining back to her and pretend that

I think Garbo is wonderful and that Donald Duck is simply
a cartoon? Never!" He gulped down some Scotch straight.
"Never!" I could not ridicule him out of his obsession. I left
him and went over to see Marcia.

I found Marcia pale, but calm, and as firm in her stand as
Gordon was in his. She insisted that he had deliberately tried
to humiliate her before that gawky so-called novelist, whose
clothes were the dowdiest she had ever seen and whose affec-
tations obviously covered up a complete lack of individuality
and intelligence. I tried to convince her that she was wrong
about Gordon's attitude at the Clarkes' party, but she said
she knew him like a book. Let him get a divorce and marry
that creature if he wanted to. They can sit around all day,
she said, and all night, too, for all I care, and talk about their
precious Donald Duck, the damn comic strip! I told Marcia
that she shouldn't allow herself to get so worked up about a
trivial and nonsensical matter. She said it was not silly and
nonsensical to her. It might have been once, yes, but it wasn't
now. It had made her see Gordon clearly for what he was,
a cheap, egotistical, resentful cad who would descend to
ridiculing his wife in front of a scrawny, horrible stranger
who could not write and never would be able to write. Furthermore, her belief in Garbo's greatness was a thing she
could not deny and would not deny, simply for the sake of
living under the same roof with Gordon Winship. The whole
thing was part and parcel of her integrity as a woman and as
an—as an, well, as a woman. She could go to work again;
he would find out.

There was nothing more that I could say or do. I went
home. That night, however, I found that I had not really
dismissed the whole ridiculous affair, as I hoped I had, for
I dreamed about it. I had tried to ignore the thing, but it had
tunnelled deeply into my subconscious. I dreamed that I was

out hunting with the Winships and that, as we crossed a snowy field, Marcia spotted a rabbit and, taking quick aim, fired and brought it down. We all ran across the snow toward the rabbit, but I reached it first. It was quite dead, but that was not what struck horror into me as I picked it up. What struck horror into me was that it was a white rabbit and was wearing a vest and carrying a watch. I woke up with a start. I don't know whether that dream means that I am on Gordon's side or on Marcia's. I don't want to analyze it. I am trying to forget the whole miserable business.

2. My Memories of D. H. Lawrence

I F YOU WANDER AROUND IN BOOKSTORES YOU WILL HAVE COME
upon several books about D. H. Lawrence: Mr. John
Middleton Murry's autobiography, Frieda Lawrence's mem-
oirs, Keith Winter's *roman à clef* called "Impassioned Pyg-
mies," etc. These are all comparatively recent; a complete
bibliography going back to the time of Lawrence's death
would run into hundreds of items, maybe thousands. The
writing man is pretty much out of it if he hasn't written something about how hard it was to understand, to talk to, and to
get along generally with D. H. Lawrence; and I do not propose to be out of it. I had my difficult moments on account
of the Master, and I intend to tell about them—if Mr. Murry
will quit talking for a moment and let me talk.

I first met D. H. Lawrence on a train platform in Italy
twelve years ago. He was pacing up and down. There was no
mistaking the reddish, scraggly beard, the dark, beetling eyebrows, the intense, restless eyes. He had the manner of a man
who was waiting for something; in this case, I think it was
the train. I had always wanted to meet the great artist and
here was my golden opportunity. I finally screwed my courage
up to the accosting point and I walked over and accosted
him. "D. H. Lawrence?" I said. He frowned, stopped, pulled
a watch out of his vest pocket, and held it up to me so that

I could see the dial. "No speak Eyetalian," he said. "Look for yourself." Then he walked away. It had been about 10:12 or 10:13 A.M. by his watch (I had 10:09 myself, but I may have been slow). Since we both got on the train that pulled into the station a few minutes later, I contrived to get into

Dr. Karns

the same compartment with him and to sit down next to him. I found him quite easy to talk to. He seemed surprised that I spoke English—on the platform he had taken me for an Italian who wanted to know what time it was. It turned out after a few minutes of rather puzzling conversation that his name was George R. Hopkins and that he had never heard of D. H. Lawrence. Hopkins was a resident of Fitchburg, Massachusetts, where he had a paper factory. He wished to God he was back in the United States. He was a strong Coolidge man, thought every French person was depraved, and hadn't been able to find a decent cup of coffee in all Europe. He had a married daughter, and two sons in Penn State, and had been having trouble with a molar in his lower jaw ever since he arrived at Le Havre, some three weeks before. He wouldn't let anybody monkey with it, he said, except a certain Dr. Karns in Fitchburg. Karns was an Elk and a bird-dog fancier in addition to being the best dentist in the United States.

This encounter did not discourage me. I determined to meet D. H. Lawrence before I came back to America, and eventually I sat down and wrote him a note, asking him for the opportunity of meeting him (I had found out where he was living at the time—in Florence, I believe, though I may be wrong). I explained that I was a great admirer of his—I addressed him simply as Dear Master—and that I had some ideas about sex which I thought might interest him. Lawrence never received the letter, it transpired later, because I had unfortunately put it in the wrong envelope. He got instead a rather sharp note which I had written the same evening to a psychoanalyst in New York who had offered to analyze me at half his usual price. This analyst had come across some sketches I had made and had apparently jumped to the conclusion that it would be interesting to try to get at what was behind them. I had addressed this man in my note simply as "sir" and I had told him that if he wanted to analyze somebody he had better begin with himself, since it was my opinion there was something the matter with him. As for me, I said, there was nothing the matter with me. This, of course, was the letter that Lawrence got, owing to the shifting of envelopes, and I was later to understand why I never heard from Lawrence and also why I kept hearing from the analyst all the time. I hung around Europe for several months waiting for a letter from Lawrence, and finally came home, in a low state of mind.

I eventually met, or rather talked with, D. H. Lawrence about six months after I got back to New York. He telephoned me one evening at my apartment. "Hello," I said into the transmitter. "Hello," a voice said. "Is this Mr. Thurber?" "Yes," I said. "Well, this is D. H. Lawrence," said the voice. I was taken back; for a moment I couldn't say a word, I was so surprised and excited. "Well, well," I said, finally, "I didn't know you were on this side." "This is the right side to be on, isn't it?" he asked, in a rather strained voice (I felt that he was excited, too). "Yes, it is," I said. "Well," said Lawrence, "they turned me over on my right side because my left side hurt me so." Thereupon he began to sing "Frankie and Johnny." He turned out to be a waggish friend of mine who had heard my stories about trying to get in touch with D. H. Lawrence, and was having me on.

I never did get to meet D. H. Lawrence, but this I rarely admit. Whenever I am at a cocktail party of literary people and the subject of Lawrence comes up, I tell my own little anecdote about the Master: how he admired Coolidge, how he had trouble with his teeth, how he liked to sing "Frankie and Johnny." These anecdotes are gaining considerable currency and I have no doubt that they will begin to creep into autobiographies of the man in a short time. Meanwhile I have become what you could almost call allergic to famous writers. I suppose this is the natural outgrowth of my curious and somewhat disturbing relationship with D. H. Lawrence. I cannot truthfully say that any part of that relationship was satisfactory, and therefore I am trying to forget D. H. Lawrence, which makes me about the only writer in the world who is. It is a distinction of a sort.

3. The Case Against Women

A BRIGHT-EYED WOMAN, WHOSE SPARKLE WAS RATHER MORE of eagerness than of intelligence, approached me at a party one afternoon and said, "Why do you hate women, Mr. Thurberg?" I quickly adjusted my fixed grin and denied that I hated women; I said I did not hate women at all. But the question remained with me, and I discovered when I went to bed that night that I had been subconsciously listing a number of reasons I do hate women. It might be interesting—at least it will help pass the time—to set down these reasons, just as they came up out of my subconscious.

In the first place, I hate women because they always know where things are. At first blush, you might think that a perverse and merely churlish reason for hating women, but it is not. Naturally, every man enjoys having a woman around the house who knows where his shirt studs and his briefcase are, and things like that, but he detests having a woman around who knows where *everything* is, even things that are of no importance at all, such as, say, the snapshots her husband took three years ago at Elbow Beach. The husband has never known where these snapshots were since the day they were developed and printed; he hopes, in a vague way, if he thinks about them at all, that after three years they have been thrown out. But his wife knows where they are, and so do his mother, his grandmother, his great-grandmother, his daughter, and the maid. They could put their fingers on them in a moment, with that quiet air of superior knowledge which makes a man feel that he is out of touch with all the things that count in life.

A man's interest in old snapshots, unless they are snapshots of himself in action with a gun, a fishing rod, or a tennis

The Cold, Flat Look

racquet, languishes in about two hours. A woman's interest in old snapshots, particularly of groups of people, never languishes; it is always there, as the years roll on, as strong and vivid as it was right at the start. She remembers the snapshots when people come to call, and just as the husband, having mixed drinks for everybody, sits down to sip his own, she will say, "George, I wish you would go and get those snapshots we took at Elbow Beach and show them to the Murphys." The husband, as I have said, doesn't know where the snapshots are; all he knows is that Harry Murphy doesn't want to see them; Harry Murphy wants to talk, just as he himself wants to talk. But Grace Murphy says that she wants to see the pictures; she is crazy to see the pictures; for one thing, the wife, who has brought the subject up, wants Mrs. Murphy to see the photo of a certain costume that the wife wore at Elbow Beach in 1933. The husband finally puts down his drink and snarls, "Well, where are they, then?" The wife, depending on her mood, gives him either the look she reserves for spoiled children or the one she reserves for drunken workmen, and tells him he knows perfectly well where they are. It turns out, after a lot of give and take, the slightly bitter edge of which is covered by forced laughs, that the snapshots are in the upper right-hand drawer of a certain desk, and the husband goes out of the room to get them. He comes back in three minutes with the news that the snapshots are not in the upper right-hand drawer of the certain desk. Without stirring from her chair, the wife favors her husband with a faint smile (the one that annoys him most of all her smiles) and reiterates that the snapshots *are* in the upper right-hand drawer of the desk. He simply didn't look, that's all. The husband knows that he looked; he knows that he prodded and dug and excavated in that drawer and that the snapshots simply are not there. The wife tells him to go look again and he will find them. The husband goes back and looks again— the guests can hear him growling and cursing and rattling papers. Then he shouts out from the next room. "They are *not* in this *drawer,* just as I told you, Ruth!" The wife quietly excuses herself and leaves the guests and goes into the room where her husband stands, hot, miserable, and defiant—and with a certain nameless fear in his heart. He has pulled the desk drawer out so far that it is about to fall on the floor, and he points at the disarray of the drawer with bitter triumph (still mixed with that nameless fear). "Look for your-self!" he snarls. The wife does not look. She says with quiet coldness, "What is that you have in your hand?" What he has in his hand turns out to be an insurance policy and an old bankbook—and the snapshots. The wife gets off the old line about what it would have done if it had been a snake, and the husband is upset for the rest of the evening; in some cases he cannot keep anything on his stomach for twenty-four hours.

Another reason I hate women (and I am speaking, I believe, for the American male generally) is that in almost every case where there is a sign reading "Please have exact change ready," a woman never has anything smaller than a ten-dollar bill. She gives ten-dollar bills to bus conductors and change men in subways and other such persons who deal in nickels and dimes and quarters. Recently, in Bermuda, I saw a woman hand the conductor on the little railway there a bill of such huge denomination that I was utterly unfamiliar with it. I was sitting too far away to see exactly what it was, but I had the feeling that it was a five-hundred-dollar bill. The con-ductor merely ignored it and stood there waiting—the fare was just one shilling. Eventually, scrabbling around in her handbag, the woman found a shilling. All the men on the train who witnessed the transaction tightened up inside; that's what a woman with a ten-dollar bill or a twenty or a five-hundred does to a man in such situations—she tightens him up inside. The episode gives him the feeling that some mon-strous triviality is threatening the whole structure of civiliza-tion. It is difficult to analyze this feeling, but there it is.

Another spectacle that depresses the male and makes him fear women, and therefore hate them, is that of a woman looking another woman up and down, to see what she is wearing. The cold, flat look that comes into a woman's eyes when she does this, the swift coarsening of her countenance, and the immediate evaporation from it of all humane quality make the male shudder. He is likely to go to his stateroom or his den or his private office and lock himself in for hours. I know one man who surprised that look in his wife's eyes and never afterward would let her come near him. If she started toward him, he would dodge behind a table or a sofa, as if he were engaging in some unholy game of tag. That look, I believe, is one reason men disappear, and turn up in Tahiti or the Arctic or the United States Navy.

I (to quit hiding behind the generalization of "the male") hate women because they almost never get anything exactly right. They say, "I have been faithful to thee, Cynara, after my fashion" instead of "in my fashion." They will bet you that Alfred Smith's middle name is Aloysius, instead of Emanuel. They will tell you to take the 2:57 train, on a day that the 2:57 does not run, or, if it does run, does not stop at the station where you are supposed to get off. Many men, separated from a woman by this particular form of imprecision, have never showed up in her life again. Nothing so embitters a man as to end up in Bridgeport when he was supposed to get off at Westport.

I hate women because they have brought into the currency of our language such expressions as "all righty" and "yes indeedy" and hundreds of others. I hate women because they throw baseballs (or plates or vases) with the wrong foot advanced. I marvel that more of them have not broken their backs. I marvel that women, who coordinate so well in languorous motion, look uglier and sillier than a goose-stepper when they attempt any form of violent activity.

I had a lot of other notes jotted down about why I hate women, but I seem to have lost them all, except one. That one is to the effect that I hate women because, while they never lose old snapshots or anything of that sort, they invariably lose one glove. I believe that I have never gone anywhere with any woman in my whole life who did not lose one glove. I have searched for single gloves under tables in crowded restaurants and under the feet of people in darkened movie theatres. I have spent some part of every day or night hunting for a woman's glove. If there were no other reason in the world for hating women, that one would be enough. In fact, you can leave all the others out.

4. No Standing Room Only

THE THEATRE PAGE OF THE "WORLD-TELEGRAM" CARRIED THIS little note one evening: "Saturday afternoon was something of an event at the Broadhurst, for 'Victoria Regina' had just rounded out fifty-two weeks on Broadway and Helen Hayes, the sentimentalist, wanted to do something to celebrate the occasion. So she called Harry Essex, the company manager, backstage and suggested that only fifty-two standees be admitted into the matinee. By curtain rise only that number of vertical playgoers were allowed into the playhouse; those turned away got no explanation from the box office."

Robert Browning says somewhere in his poems that Providence often seems to "let twenty pass and stone the twenty-first." Miss Hayes goes Providence thirty-two better and thus is about two and a half times as lenient. She didn't have the fifty-third man stoned, either, or otherwise roughly handled, but he must have been just about as bewildered and sore as if he had been. To celebrate the anniversary of a popular play by refusing to let certain people in to see it sets a new precedent for celebrations, particularly sentimental celebrations. I somehow have the idea that Harry Essex, the company manager, didn't really understand what Miss Hayes said. I think she probably suggested that the first fifty-two persons who asked for standing room be let in free. That's more along the old, established lines of celebration and sentiment, and sounds more like Miss Hayes, somehow. I don't know whether it sounds like Mr. Essex or not, but I imagine

it doesn't. I never heard of a company manager who would let fifty-two people in free; on the other hand, I never heard of one who would keep people out when they wanted to pay to get in. Of course, it may be that the box-office man got mixed up on his instructions, but that doesn't sound like a box-office man. I don't suppose we will ever get to the bottom of it all, but I can't help wondering what happened when the fifty-third person showed up and wanted to pay to get into the show. Let us try to reconstruct his conversation with the box-office man:

MR. FIFTY-THREE: I want a ticket, please.

BOX-OFFICE MAN: Standing room only.

MR. FIFTY-THREE: All right, give me standing room.

BOX-OFFICE MAN: But—uh—I just remembered—there is standing room but I can't sell you any.

MR. FIFTY-THREE: What did you say?

BOX-OFFICE MAN: I say there is standing room but I can't sell you any.

MR. FIFTY-THREE: I don't get it. It sounds as if you kept saying there is standing room but you can't sell me any.

BOX-OFFICE MAN: That's what I said.

MR. FIFTY-THREE: Well, say it again. Some other way.

BOX-OFFICE MAN: All I have is no standing room. No standing room only.

MR. FIFTY-THREE: Huh?

BOX-OFFICE MAN: Look—if you come back *next* Saturday, or even tonight, I could let you in even if it were more crowded in there than it is now, but I can't tell you why.

MR. FIFTY-THREE: I want to get in now. I'd rather stand when there are fewer standees.

BOX-OFFICE MAN: I can't let you in.

MR. FIFTY-THREE: Why can't you?

BOX-OFFICE MAN: I just can't, that's all.

MR. FIFTY-THREE: What's the matter with me?

BOX-OFFICE MAN: Nothing's the matter with you.

MR. FIFTY-THREE: Well, something must be the matter with somebody.

BOX-OFFICE MAN: No, nothing's the matter, exactly.

MR. FIFTY-THREE: Well, *approximately,* what's the matter?

BOX-OFFICE MAN: I can't sell you a ticket to stand.

MR. FIFTY-THREE: You sold the man right ahead of me standing room, because I saw you.

BOX-OFFICE MAN: If he'd been behind you, *you* could have got in, but *he* couldn't.

MR. FIFTY-THREE: Are you Charles MacArthur?

BOX-OFFICE MAN: No.

MR. FIFTY-THREE: Why? Why? Why?

BOX-OFFICE MAN: Because I'm not.

MR. FIFTY-THREE: No, no, I mean why can't I *get in?*

BOX-OFFICE MAN: I can't tell you. I can't give any explanation.

MR. FIFTY-THREE: Do you *know* why I can't get in?

BOX-OFFICE MAN: I don't want to talk about it.

By this time, Mrs. Fifty-Four and Mrs. Fifty-five, and a lot of other women on up to Mrs. Seventy-two, are pushing, and they finally dislodge Mr. Fifty-three and demand standing room. The box-office man has to get rid of them, which is harder than getting rid of Mr. Fifty-three, lots harder. Just how many bewildered people were turned away in all on this sentimental occasion, I don't know, but I'm glad I wasn't the box-office man.

The American Airlines, now, has the good old-fashioned idea of celebrating a sentimental occasion. They recently decided to give a prize to the millionth person who chanced to show up and ask for passage on one of their planes. Up showed the lucky Mr. Theodore Colcord Baker. He was given a free trip to Europe on the Hindenburg and a thousand dollars in cash. It would take a hundred thousand dollars to get me to ride on the Hindenburg or any other Zeppelin, but that is beside the point. The point is that when Mr. Baker showed up he wasn't told that American Airlines wouldn't let him ride on one of their planes. The sentiment of that would have been lost on Mr. Baker, even if it had been explained to him. It would have been lost on Miss Hayes and Mr. Essex, too, particularly if they were in a hurry to fly somewhere. Of course, if Mr. Fifty-three had been in a hurry to see "Victoria Regina" he probably wouldn't have waited a year, but the sentiment in both cases is the same. I'm not trying to compare a plane ride to a matinée, I'm trying to compare Helen Hayes to American Airlines; even so, I would be the last to say that Miss Hayes should have given anyone a thousand dollars. I just think she should have let Mr. Fifty-three in.

I've brooded about this affair for quite a few days and nights now, and out of it I have hit on a kind of revenge for Mr. Fifty-three, if he still is as mad as I think he is. My plan would be hard to work but it would be a lot of fun. In "Victoria Regina," as you know, Prince Albert dies, rather early in the play. Now my idea is to have Mr. Fifty-three, if he has any spunk at all, don the uniform of a court announcer some Saturday afternoon, put on makeup, slip backstage when nobody is looking, and, in the scene after Albert's death, walk boldly onstage and, with a gesture toward the door, say, loudly, "The Royal Consort, Prince Albert!" They would either have to ring the curtain down or else Mr. Vincent Price, who plays Prince Albert, would have to walk on again, as fit as a fiddle but with nothing to say, except maybe that he was feeling a lot better than he had been. That would put Miss Hayes in a very sentimental spot. But perhaps I have brooded about the whole business too long. I guess I have.

5. Nine Needles

ONE OF THE MORE SPECTACULAR MINOR HAPPENINGS OF THE past few years which I am sorry that I missed took place in the Columbus, Ohio, home of some friends of a friend of mine. It seems that a Mr. Albatross, while looking for something in his medicine cabinet one morning, discovered a bottle of a kind of patent medicine which his wife had been taking for a stomach ailment. Now, Mr. Albatross is one of those apprehensive men who are afraid of patent medicines and of almost everything else. Some weeks before, he had encountered a paragraph in a Consumers' Research bulletin which announced that this particular medicine was bad for you. He had thereupon ordered his wife to throw out what was left of her supply of the stuff and never buy any more. She had promised, and here now was another bottle of the perilous liquid. Mr. Albatross, a man given to quick rages, shouted the conclusion of the story at my friend: "I threw the bottle out the bathroom window and the medicine chest after it!" It seems to me that must have been a spectacle worth going a long way to see.

I am sure that many a husband has wanted to wrench the family medicine cabinet off the wall and throw it out the window, if only because the average medicine cabinet is so filled with mysterious bottles and unidentifiable objects of all kinds that it is a source of constant bewilderment and exasperation to the American male. Surely the British medicine cabinet and the French medicine cabinet and all the other

"And the Medicine Chest After It!"

medicine cabinets must be simpler and better ordered than ours. It may be that the American habit of saving everything and never throwing anything away, even empty bottles, causes the domestic medicine cabinet to become as cluttered in its small way as the American attic becomes cluttered in its major way. I have encountered few medicine cabinets in this country which were not pack-jammed with something between a hundred and fifty and two hundred different items, from dental floss to boracic acid, from razor blades to sodium perborate, from adhesive tape to coconut oil. Even the neatest wife will put off clearing out the medicine cabinet on the ground that she has something else to do that is more important at the moment, or more diverting. It was in the apartment of such a wife and her husband that I became enormously involved with a medicine cabinet one morning not long ago.

I had spent the weekend with this couple—they live on East Tenth Street near Fifth Avenue—such a weekend as left me reluctant to rise up on Monday morning with bright and shining face and go to work. They got up and went to work, but I didn't. I didn't get up until about two-thirty in the afternoon. I had my face all lathered for shaving and the washbowl was full of hot water when suddenly I cut myself with the razor. I cut my ear. Very few men cut their ears with razors, but I do, possibly because I was taught the old Spencerian free-wrist movement by my writing teacher in the grammar grades. The ear bleeds rather profusely when cut with a razor and is difficult to get at. More angry than hurt, I jerked open the door of the medicine cabinet to see if I could find a styptic pencil and out fell, from the top shelf, a little black paper packet containing nine needles. It seems that this wife kept a little paper packet containing nine needles on the top shelf of the medicine cabinet. The packet fell into the soapy water of the washbowl, where the paper rapidly disintegrated, leaving nine needles at large in the bowl. I was, naturally enough, not in the best condition, either physical or mental, to recover nine needles from a washbowl. No gentleman who has lather on his face and whose ear is bleeding is in the best condition for anything, even something involving the handling of nine large blunt objects.

It did not seem wise to me to pull the plug out of the washbowl and let the needles go down the drain. I had visions of clogging up the plumbing system of the house, and also a vague fear of causing short circuits somehow or other (I know very little about electricity and I don't want to have it explained to me). Finally, I groped very gently around the bowl and eventually had four of the needles in the palm of one hand and three in the palm of the other—two I couldn't find. If I had thought quickly and clearly, I wouldn't have done that. A lathered man whose ear is bleeding and who has four wet needles in one hand and three in the other may be said to have reached the lowest known point of human efficiency. There is nothing he can do but stand there. I tried transferring the needles in my left hand to the palm of my right hand, but I couldn't get them off my left hand. Wet needles cling to you. In the end, I wiped the needles off onto a bathtowel which was hanging on a rod above the bathtub. It was the only towel that I could find. I had to dry my hands afterward on the bathmat. Then I tried to find the needles in the towel. Hunting for seven needles in a bathtowel is the most tedious occupation I have ever engaged in. I could find only five of them. With the two that had been left in the bowl, that meant there were four needles in all missing— two in the washbowl and two others lurking in the towel or lying in the bathtub under the towel. Frightful thoughts came to me of what might happen to anyone who used that towel or washed his face in the bowl or got into the tub, if I didn't find the missing needles. Well, I didn't find them. I sat down on the edge of the tub to think, and I decided finally that the only thing to do was wrap up the towel in a newspaper and take it away with me. I also decided to leave a note for my friends explaining as clearly as I could that I was afraid there were two needles in the bathtub and two needles in the washbowl, and that they better be careful.

I looked everywhere in the apartment, but I could not find a pencil, or a pen, or a typewriter. I could find pieces of paper, but nothing with which to write on them. I don't know what gave me the idea—a movie I had seen, perhaps, or a story I had read—but I suddenly thought of writing a message with a lipstick. The wife might have an extra lipstick lying around and, if so, I concluded it would be in the medicine cabinet. I went back to the medicine cabinet and began poking around in it for a lipstick. I saw what I thought looked like the metal tip of one, and I got two fingers around it and began to pull gently—it was under a lot of things. Every object in the medicine cabinet began to slide. Bottles broke in the washbowl and on the floor; red, brown, and white liquids spurted; nail files, scissors, razor blades, and miscellaneous objects sang and clattered and tinkled. I was covered with perfume, peroxide, and cold cream.

It took me half an hour to get the debris all together in the middle of the bathroom floor. I made no attempt to put anything back in the medicine cabinet. I knew it would take a steadier hand than mine and a less shattered spirit. Before I went away (only partly shaved) and abandoned the shambles, I left a note saying that I was afraid there were needles in the bathtub and the washbowl and that I had taken their towel and that I would call up and tell them everything—I wrote it in iodine with the end of a toothbrush. I have not yet called up, I am sorry to say. I have neither found the courage nor thought up the words to explain what happened. I suppose my friends believe that I deliberately smashed up their bathroom and stole their towel. I don't know for sure, because they have not yet called me up, either.

6. A Couple of Hamburgers

IT HAD BEEN RAINING FOR A LONG TIME, A SLOW, COLD RAIN falling out of iron-colored clouds. They had been driving since morning and they still had a hundred and thirty miles to go. It was about three o'clock in the afternoon. "I'm getting hungry," she said. He took his eyes off the wet, winding road for a fraction of a second and said, "We'll stop at a dog-wagon." She shifted her position irritably. "I wish you wouldn't call them *dog*-wagons," she said. He pressed the klaxon button and went around a slow car. "That's what they are," he said. "Dog-wagons." She waited a few seconds. "*Decent* people call them *diners*," she told him, and added, "Even if you call them diners, I don't like them." He speeded up a hill. "They have better stuff than most restaurants," he said. "Anyway, I want to get home before dark and it takes too long in a restaurant. We can stay our stomachs with a couple hamburgers." She lighted a cigarette and he asked her to light one for him. She lighted one deliberately and handed it to him. "I wish you wouldn't say 'stay our stomachs,'" she said. "You know I hate that. It's like 'sticking to your ribs.' You say that all the time." He grinned. "Good old American expressions, both of them," he said. "Like sow belly. Old pioneer term, sow belly." She sniffed. "My ancestors were pioneers, too. You don't have to be vulgar just because you were a pioneer." "Your ancestors never got as far west as mine did," he said. "The real pioneers travelled on their sow belly and got somewhere." He laughed loudly at that. She looked out at the wet trees and signs and telephone poles going by. They drove on for several miles without a word; he kept chortling every now and then.

"What's that funny sound?" she asked, suddenly. It invariably made him angry when she heard a funny sound. "What funny sound?" he demanded. "You're always hearing

funny sounds." She laughed briefly. "That's what you said when the bearing burned out," she reminded him. "You'd never have noticed it if it hadn't been for me." "I noticed it, all right," he said. "Yes," she said. "When it was too late." She enjoyed bringing up the subject of the burned-out bearing whenever he got to chortling. "It was too late when *you* noticed it, as far as that goes," he said. Then, after a pause, "Well, what does it sound like *this* time? All engines make a noise running, you know." "I know all about that," she answered. "It sounds like—it sounds like a lot of safety pins being jiggled around in a tumbler." He snorted. "That's your imagination. Nothing gets the matter with a car that sounds like a lot of safety pins. I happen to know that." She tossed away her cigarette. "Oh, sure," she said. "You always happen to know everything." They drove on in silence.

"I want to stop somewhere and get something to *eat*!" she said loudly. "All right, all right!" he said. "I been watching for a dog-wagon, haven't I? There hasn't been any. I can't make you a dog-wagon." The wind blew rain in on her and she put up the window on her side all the way. "I won't stop at just any old diner," she said. "I won't stop unless it's a cute one." He looked around at her. "Unless it's a *what* one?" he shouted. "You know what I mean," she said. "I mean a decent, clean one where they don't slosh things at you. I hate to have a lot of milky coffee sloshed at me." "All right," he said. "We'll find a cute one, then. You pick it out. I wouldn't know. I might find one that was cunning but not cute." That struck him as funny and he began to chortle again. "Oh, shut up," she said.

Five miles farther along they came to a place called Sam's Diner. "Here's one," he said, slowing down. She looked it over. "I don't want to stop there," she said. "I don't like the ones that have nicknames." He brought the car to a stop at one side of the road. "Just what's the matter with the ones that have nicknames?" he asked with edgy, mock interest. "They're always Greek ones," she told him. "They're always Greek ones," he repeated after her. He set his teeth firmly together and started up again. After a time, "Good old Sam, the Greek," he said, in a singsong. "Good old Connecticut Sam Beardsley, the Greek." "You didn't see his name," she snapped. "Winthrop, then," he said. "Old Samuel Cabot Winthrop, the Greek dog-wagon man." He was getting hungry.

On the outskirts of the next town she said, as he slowed down, "It looks like a factory kind of town." He knew that she meant she wouldn't stop there. He drove on through the place. She lighted a cigarette as they pulled out into the open again. He slowed down and lighted a cigarette for himself. "Factory kind of town than *I* am!" he snarled. It was ten miles before they came to another town. "Torrington," he growled. "Happen to know there's a dog-wagon here because I stopped in it once with Bob Combs. Damn cute place, too, if you ask me." "I'm not asking you anything," she said, coldly. "You think you're *so* funny. I think I know the one you mean," she said, after a moment. "It's right in the town and it sits at an angle from the road. They're never so good, for some reason." He glared at her and almost ran up against the curb. "What the hell do you mean 'sits at an angle from the road'?" he cried. He was very hungry now. "Well, it isn't silly," she said, calmly. "I've noticed the ones that sit at an angle. They're cheaper, because they fitted them into funny little pieces of ground. The big ones parallel to the road are the best." He drove right through Torrington, his lips compressed. "Angle from the *road*, for God's sake!" he snarled, finally. She was looking out her window.

On the outskirts of the next town there was a diner called The Elite Diner. "This looks—" she began. "I see it, I see it!" he said. "It doesn't happen to look any cuter to me than any goddam—" she cut him off. "Don't be such a sorehead, for Lord's sake," she said. He pulled up and stopped beside the diner, and turned on her. "Listen," he said, grittingly, "I'm going to put down a couple of hamburgers in this place even if there isn't one single inch of chintz or cretonne in the whole—" "Oh, be still," she said. "You're just hungry and mean like a child. Eat your old hamburgers, what do I care?" Inside the place they sat down on stools and the counterman walked over to them, wiping up the counter top with a cloth as he did so. "What'll it be, folks?" he said. "Bad day, ain't it? Except for ducks." "I'll have a couple of—" began the husband, but his wife cut in. "I just want a pack of cigarettes," she said. He turned around slowly on his stool and stared at her as she put a dime and a nickel in the cigarette machine and ejected a package of Lucky Strikes. He turned to the counterman again. "I want a couple of hamburgers," he said. "With mustard and lots of onion. *Lots* of onion!" She hated onions. "I'll wait for you in the car," she said. He didn't answer and she went out.

He finished his hamburgers and his coffee slowly. It was terrible coffee. Then he went out to the car and got in and drove off, slowly humming "Who's Afraid of the Big Bad Wolf?" After a mile or so, "Well," he said, "what was the matter with the Elite Diner, milady?" "Didn't you *see* that cloth the man was wiping the counter with?" she demanded. "Ugh!" She shuddered. "I didn't happen to want to eat any of the counter," he said. He laughed at that comeback. "You didn't even notice it," she said. "You never notice anything. It was filthy." "I noticed they had some damn fine coffee in there," he said. "It was swell." He knew she loved good coffee. He began to hum his tune again; then he whistled it; then he began to sing it. She did not show her annoyance, but she knew that he knew she was annoyed. "Will you be kind enough to tell me what time it is?" she asked. "Big *bad* wolf, big *bad* wolf—five minutes o' five—tum-dee-*doo*-dee-dum-m-m." She settled back in her seat and took a cigarette from her case and tapped it on the case. "I'll wait till we get home," she said. "If you'll be kind enough to speed up a little." He drove on at the same speed. After a time he gave up the "Big Bad Wolf" and there was deep silence for two miles. Then suddenly he began to sing, very loudly,

H-A-double-R-*I*-G-A-*N* *spells Harrr*-i-gan—" She gritted her teeth. She hated that worse than any of his songs except "Barney Google." He would go on to "Barney Google" pretty soon, she knew. Suddenly she leaned slighty forward. The straight line of her lips began to curve up ever so slightly. She heard the safety pins in the tumbler again. Only now they were louder, more insistent, ominous. He was singing too loud to hear them. "Is a *name* that *shame* has never been con-*nec*-ted with—*Harrr*-i-gan, that's *me!*" She relaxed against the back of the seat, content to wait.

7. The Case of the Laughing Butler

A LADY WHO SIGNED HERSELF "HOSTESS" WROTE RECENTLY TO Elinor Ames, who clears up matters of etiquette for the distraught readers of the *Daily News,* "How many cocktails should a hostess serve before a meal? Sometimes I feel so embarrassed because the dinner is ready but the guests go right on drinking in the living room and I can't find a tactful way to urge them out to dinner. I have no maid so must announce dinner myself." To which Miss Ames replied, "Never serve more than two cocktails before dinner, for the guest who has several cocktails and an assortment of canapés and hors-d'œuvre will suffer a loss of appetite. Why not try a laughing imitation of a bûtler? Stand at the door and say, in clear tones, 'Dinner is served.' If your manner is pleasant but pointed—and there are no more cocktails—your guests will follow you into the dining room."

Here we have stated, by Hostess, one of the problems of American home life today, and one which you and I—and, in her hearts of hearts, Miss Ames herself—know cannot be solved by imitating a butler. One might as well try to dispose of some such problem as "What shall one do about sex?" by imitating a butler. To give a brief history of cocktails-before-dinner, every school child knows, of course, that the trouble began when liquor was substituted for tea as a late-

To Enjoy Imitations People Must Have about Five Cocktails

afternoon and early-evening beverage. The old-fashioned tea party was easy to handle; your Aunt Clara or your little neice could handle it, and have the whole house in apple-pie order again by half past six. Nobody ever drank more than one or two cups of tea (three at the outside), and even if he did it had no other effect than to make him slightly stupid. There was never any disposition on the part of tea drinkers to go on and on with the thing; nobody ever crept into the guest room and lay down; nobody shouted. I do not pretend that such things occur at all parties where cocktails are served; what I mean to say is that they never occurred at tea parties. The tea party could be decorous to the point of stuffiness, it had all the drawbacks of the stone-sober, but it was eminently manageable. Then came, as we all know, gin, and with it the problem with which Hostess finds herself confronted.

The weakness of Miss Ames' attempt to cope with the cocktail problem, the proof of her uncertainty and lack of confidence in her own plan, lies in that curious suggestion of hers, "Why not try a laughing imitation of a butler?" If she had had any faith in her ability to help Hostess out, she would not have answered a hard question by asking another question. Well, let me answer that question for Hostess, who must be pretty bewildered. In the first place, if a hostess stands at the door and laughs, nobody is going to get the idea that she is imitating a butler, for the simple reason that butlers do not laugh. You have to give an unsmiling and dignified imitation of a butler or the whole thing falls flat. Furthermore, it is extremely difficult for a woman in a dinner gown to imitate a butler. I doubt if any woman except Beatrice Lillie could get away with it, and she probably has a butler. (Miss Ames' implication that the presence of an actual butler would solve the cocktail problem we need not bother with here further than to say it wouldn't.) Moreover, a roomful of guests who have had only two cocktails are not going to be amused by, or cater to, anybody doing imitations of any kind whatsoever. To enjoy imitations, or even pay attention to imitations, people must have about five cocktails, at which point they will, of course, begin giving imitations themselves— the gentleman with mustaches doing Hitler and Charlie Chaplin. Gentlemen—or ladies—imitating Chaplin are likely to be a nuisance in a crowded room, particularly if they try going around a corner on one foot. Getting people who are doing imitations out to the dining room would be next to impossible.

But let us, for the sake of the argument, consider Miss Ames' specific case, that of a hostess who, having served two cocktails and determining not to serve any more, stands at the door and gives a laughing imitation of a butler. Nothing, beyond a few strained little laughs, is going to happen. The hostess is simply going to stand there, her idiotic laughter dying, while a roomful of people, each holding his empty glass rigidly before him, regard their hostess with cold grins. There is only one thing for Hostess to do at this point, and I shall express it by paraphrasing one of Miss Ames' own sentences, as follows: "If your manner is pleasant but pointed— and there are no more cocktails—you are going to have to make some more cocktails." This has become the accepted thing, and there is nothing to do but accept it. Dinner can always wait for one more round, or if it can't, it is going to, anyway.

There is really only one way for a hostess to speed her guests to the dinner table after two cocktails, but it is a remedy that is worse than the malady. I refer to the serving of purple or blue cocktails or cocktails of any color not ordinarily encountered in liquor glasses. Strangely colored cocktails, made up of liquid odds and ends, can be, and often are, served by women like Hostess. As Marjorie Hillis says in "Live Alone and Like It," "Worse even than the woman who puts marshmallows into a salad is the one who goes in for fancy cocktails." (Miss Hillis knows quite a lot about serving drinks, but she has a one-cocktail delusion about Old-Fashioneds. She writes, "Old-Fashioneds come into the economy class after a fashion, because of the fact that you make them singly, and *usually people don't expect two*." I believe it can safely be said that nothing in the world depresses a guest so much as only one Old-Fashioned.) The serving of fancy cocktails, then—to get back to the fancy cocktails—is one way out for Hostess. It will be an even better way out if she serves with them canapés made of anchovy paste mixed with marmalade, or something of the sort, and gives each gentleman a dainty little cocktail napkin to worry about. This will get the guests out to dinner all right but it will also get them out of the house right after dinner, probably never to return. There don't have to be any marshmallows in the salad. Thus we see that there is no perfect, or even near-perfect, solution to Hostess's problem in this country.

In France our problem does not come up because the French look on cocktails before dinner as an invention of the devil (*une invention du diable*). No proper French person would ever let himself in for any such quandary as confronts Hostess; first, because it is repugnant to the French to dull the palate with gin and rye, thus spoiling the taste for food, and, second, because it costs too much (*c'est trop cher*). Many Americans have no real taste for food, or, if they have, they are so worried or nervous by late afternoon that they don't care. Thus it has come about that a great number of Americans, instead of giving up cocktails before dinner, are largely giving up dinner after cocktails. A professor out in Ohio has announced that because of this Americans are rapidly becoming a one-meal race, having the time and inclination only for a cup of coffee and a piece of toast in the morning. The professor's conclusion seems to be that when the barbarians come down from the North they will find a people so badly nourished that they will be a pushover.

I happen to be an old-fashioned host who does not believe in the abandonment of dinner after cocktails. This is probably because I rarely have a chance to have more than one cocktail at my own dinner parties, owing to the fact that I usually have to go out for ice, and hence have just worked up an appetite when dinner is announced, or by the time it should be announced. Dinner guests have a way of showing up at my house quite early, bringing anywhere from one to six people with them. Sometimes it is somebody's father who just wanted to stop in and see me before he took his train; sometimes it is four or five friends of one of my guests, with whom he has been having a quick one at Joe's or somewhere, and who thought they would just drop in and say hello; sometimes it is that bald man with the nose glasses and that middle-aged woman in the brown dress who so often show up at people's houses at five-thirty or six o'clock. In these cases the ice, of course, runs out and I have to go out and get some more (the ice-cube system is not, I believe, here to stay, unless it gets a great deal better). Thus I usually find myself over in Bleecker or Sullivan Street at seven o'clock of the evening I am giving a dinner party, trying to explain to some Italian that I have to have ice. Of course, I usually try to phone for the ice first, but that never works, as you know if you have tried it. You can get Tony Angelli or Tony Dibello on the phone, all right, but you can't make him understand that you want ice. You say, "Hello—Angelli's?," and a thick, low voice says, "Hodda wodda poosh?" "Could you deliver some ice right away to such-and-such a number?"

you ask, above the racket of the cocktail drinkers. "You gudda poosh what?" says the voice. You never really get beyond that, whatever it is, so you have to go out for the ice. It is useless to send a servant. No servant has ever been known to find an Italian ice-dealer.

On one occasion I waited for half an hour in the steamy kitchen of a house in Sullivan Street until the Italian ice-man, who had disappeared after a brief and excited talk with me, came back with some white wine. He had thought I wanted white wine. Is was very late when I got back with the ice that time and everybody had a good laugh at me, to be sure, coming in with the ice. When I go out for the ice now, I usually snatch a couple of sandwiches at a delicatessen. It isn't much, but it is something. My own experience is simply one example of why it is impossible to solve the cocktails-before-dinner problem as glibly and briefly as Miss Ames tries to solve it. I don't like to think of Hostess standing there at the door, laughingly imitating a butler, hoping everybody will clap hands and file gaily out to dinner. Life isn't that simple.

8. Bateman Comes Home

(Written After Reading Several Recent Novels about the Deep South and Confusing them a Little—as the Novelists Themselves Do—with "Tobacco Road" and "God's Little Acre")

OLD NATE BIRGE SAT ON THE RUSTED WRECK OF AN ANCIENT sewing machine in front of Hell Fire, which was what his shack was known as among the neighbors and to the police. He was chewing on a splinter of wood and watching the moon come up lazily out of the old cemetery in which nine of his daughters were lying, only two of whom were dead. He began to mutter to himself. "Bateman be comin' back any time now wid a thousan' dollas fo' his ol' pappy," said Birge. "Bateman ain' goin' let his ol' pappy starve nohow." A high, cracked voice spoke inside the house, in a toneless singsong. "Bateman see you in hell afore he do anything 'bout it," said the voice. "Who dat?" cried Birge, standing up. "Who dat sayin' callumy 'bout Bateman? Good gahd amighty!" He sat down quickly again. His feet hurt him, since he had gangrene in one of them and Bless-Yo-Soul, the cow, had stepped on the other one that morning in Hell Hole, the pasture behind Hell Fire. A woman came to the door with a skillet in her hand. Elviry Birge was thin and emaciated and dressed in a tattered old velvet evening gown. "You oughtn' speak thataway 'bout Bateman at thisatime," said Birge. "Bateman's a good boy. He go 'way in 1904 to make his pappy a thousan' dollas." "Thuh hell wuth thut," said

Elviry, even more tonelessly than usual. "Bateman ain' goin'
brang we-all no thousan' dollas. Bateman got heself a place
fo' dat thousan' dollas." She shambled back into the house.
"Elviry's gone crazy," muttered Birge to himself.

A large woman with a heavy face walked into the littered
yard, followed by a young man dressed in a tight blue suit.
The woman carried two suitcases; the young man was smoking a cigarette and running a pocket comb through his hair.
"Who dat?" demanded Birge, peering into the dark. "It's
me, yore Sister Sairy," said the large woman. "An' tuckered
as a truck horse." The young man threw his cigarette on the
ground and spat at its burning end. "Mom shot a policeman
in Chicago," he said, sulkily, "an' we hadda beat it." "Whut
you shoot a policeman fo', Sairy?" demanded Birge, who had
not seen his sister for twenty years. "Gahdam it, you cain' go
'round doin' that!" "That'll be one o' Ramsay's jokes," said
Sairy. "Ramsay's a hand for jokes, he is. Seems like that's
all he *is* a hand for." "Ah, shut yore trap before I slap it shut,"
said Ramsay. He had never been in the deep South before and
he didn't like it. "When do we eat?" he asked. "Ev'body goin'
'round shootin' policemen," muttered Birge, hobbling about
the yard. "Seem lak ev'body shootin' policeman 'cept Bateman. Bateman, he's a good boy." Elviry came to the door
again, still carrying the skillet; as they had had no food since
Coolidge's first term, she used it merely as a weapon. "Whut's
ut?" she asked, frowning into the dark. The moon, grown
tired, had sunk back into the cemetery again. "Come ahn out,
cackle-puss, an' find out," said Ramsay. "Look heah, boy!"
cried Birge. "I want me more rev'rence outa you, gahdam it!"
"Hello, Elviry," said Sairy, sitting on one of her suitcases. "We
come to visit you. Ain't you glad?" Elviry didn't move from
the doorway.

"We-all thought you-all was in *She*cago," said Elviry, in her toneless voice. "We-all was in all Chicago," said Ramsay, "but we-all is here all, now all." He spat. "Dam ef he ain' right, too," said Birge, chuckling. "Lawdy gahd! You bring me a a thousan' dollas, boy?" he asked, suddenly. "I ain't brought nobody no thousand dollers," growled Ramsay. "Whine you make yerself a thousand dollers, you old buzzard?" "Don' lem call me buzzard, Elviry!" shouted Birge. "Cain' you hit him wid somethin'? Hit him wid dat skillet!" Elviry made for Ramsay with her skillet, but he wrested it away from her and struck her over the head with it. The impact made a low, dull sound, like *sponk*. Elviry fell unconscious, and Ramsay sat down on her, listlessly. "Hell va place ya got here," he said.

At this juncture a young blonde girl, thin and emaciated but beautiful in the light of the moon (which had come up again), ran into the yard. "Wheah you bin, gal?" demanded Birge. "Faith is crazy," he said to the others, "an' they ain' nobody knows why, 'cause I give her a good Christian upbringin' ef evah a man did. Look heah, gal, yo' Aunt Sairy heah fo' a visit, gahdam it, an' nobody home to welcome her. All my daughters 'cept Prudence bin gone fo' two weeks now. Prudence, she bin gone fo' two yeahs." Faith sat down on the stoop. "Clay an' me bin settin' fire to the auditorium," she said. Birge began whittling at a stick. "Clay's her third husban'," he said. "'Pears lak she should pay some 'tention to her fifth husban', or leastwise her fo'th, but she don'. I don' understan' wimmin. Seem lak ev'body settin' fire to somethin' ev'time I turn my back. Wonder any buildin's standin' in the whole gahdam United States. You see anythin' o' Bateman, gal?" "I ain' seen anythin' o' anybody," said Faith. "Now that is a bald-face lie by a daughter I brought up in the feah o' hell fire," said Birge. "Look heah, gal, you cain' set fire to no buildin' 'thout you see somebody. Gahd's love give that truth to this world. Speak to yo' Aunt Sairy, gal. She jest kill hesef a *po*liceman in *She*cago." "Did you kill a policeman, Aunt Sairy?" Faith asked her. Sairy didn't answer her, but she spoke to Ramsay. "You sit on this suitcase an' let me sit on Elviry a while," she said. "Do as yo' Motha tells you boy," said Birge. "Ah, shut up!" said Ramsay, smoking.

Ben Turnip, a half-witted neighbor boy with double pneumonia, came into the yard, wearing only overalls. "Ah seed you-all was a-settin'," he said, bursting into high, toneless laughter. "Heah's Bateman! Heah's Bateman!" cried Birge, hobbling with many a painful gahdam over to the newcomer. "You bring me a thousan' dollas, Bateman?" Elviry came to, pushed Ramsay off her, and got up. "That ain' Bateman, you ol' buzzard," she said, scornfully. "That's only Ben Turnip an' him turned in the haid, too, lak his Motha afore him." "Go 'long, woman," said Birge. "I reckon I know moan son. You bring yo' ol' pappy a thousan' dollas, Bateman?" "Ah seed you-all was a-settin'," said Ben Turnip. Suddenly he became very excited, his voice rising to a high singsong. "He-settin', I-settin', you-settin', we-settin'," he screamed. "Deed-a-bye, deed-a-bye, deed-a-bye, die!" "Bateman done gone crazy," mumbled Birge. He went back and sat down on the sewing machine. "Seem lak ev'body gone crazy. Now, that's a pity," he said, sadly. "Nuts," said Ramsay.

"S'pose you-all did see me a-settin'," said Ben Turnip, belligerently. "Whut uv ut? Cain' Ah set?" "Sho, sho, set yosef, Bateman," said Birge. "I'll whang ovah his haid wid Elviry's skillet fust pusson say anything 'bout you settin'. Set yosef." Ben sat down on the ground and began digging with a stick. "I done brong you a thousan' dollas," said Ben. Birge leaped from his seat. "Glory gahd to Hallerlugie!" he shouted. "You heah de man, Elviry? Bateman done . . ."

If you keep on long enough it turns into a novel.

9. Footnotes on a Course of Study

I HARDLY KNOW WHERE TO BEGIN IN TRYING TO SUMMARIZE FOR you a pamphlet called "The Technique of Good Manners," by one Mary Perin Barker, which has fallen into my hands. I might begin, I suppose, by saying that it was first got up to be used, and was used, as a course of study at Newark College of Engineering, but that would only start you asking questions, and all I know is that Newark College of Engineering is a college. Mrs. Barker's little book was devised to instruct the men students there how to act from the time they got up until the time they went to bed. These students used to meet with the author for two-hour discussion periods; whether they still do or not I don't know; at any rate, the brochure has now been put into general circulation, with an introductory note by Dr. Dexter S. Kimball, Dean of the College of Engineering of Cornell University. Mrs. Barker teaches proper behavior in the classroom, the ballroom, the laboratory, and the office. She tells you how to answer the phone (you should never grab it up and shout "Yeah?"), how to take a girl to a dance, how to greet one's office mates (you say "Hello there," with a smile, and "mean it"), and so on.

Being a woman, Mrs. Barker goes into italics in surprising places now and then. For instance, she writes, early in this course of study, that a man should have "a razor, a *good* hairbrush, a toothbrush, and a pants presser." Well, that's a woman for you, putting the quality of a hairbrush above the quality of a razor. Somehow, I can just see the razor she has in mind, and the hairbrush too, as far as that goes. I don't want any part of either one of them. I don't care whether I'm well groomed or not. I don't want to be groomed, anyway;

For Cleaning Shoes There Is Nothing so Handy as a Handkerchief

never have. I just want to get up and dress and be let alone. This makes me a boor, I know, and Mrs. Barker, being a cultivated lady (she believes that men should shave under their arms and points out that "for years they have done so at the foreign beach resorts"), Mrs. Barker hates a boor, but we all might as well know where we stand to begin with. It just happens that I do practically nothing the way Mrs. Barker says it should be done. For one thing, I usually argue with people when my clothes are rumpled and my hair is in my eyes. Mrs. B. intimates that you get much farther if you are well dressed. She writes, "One friend of mine says that she never starts an argument unless she is well dressed." I know women like that, too, and they're just as well dressed at the end as they were when they started. And yet nothing so upsets the ill-groomed man as to have a woman come out of an argument with him just as well groomed as when she went in, and talking in the same cool tones, with the same faint smile on her lips. I know them.

To go on to other items in Mrs. Barker's code of behavior for men, she says that it is entirely out of place to use handkerchiefs to "clean shoes, to dust furniture, or to wipe automobile grease or laboratory acid from the hands." I don't know about the automobile grease or the laboratory acid, and I don't care about the furniture-dusting, but I do know that for cleaning shoes there is nothing so handy or so efficient as a handkerchief. The handkerchief a man uses on his shoes he can always tuck away quickly in his pocket where his wife can't see it; on the way to the office he can toss it into a trash receptacle. If he uses a towel, on the other hand, his wife is bound to find it, confront him with it, and say, "What have you been doing with this, may I ask—dipping sheep?" That is likely to ruin the man's day.

As to table manners, I concede most of Mrs. Barker's points, but I cannot go the whole way with her about introductions. She contends that in introducing people a clue to their interests is often a kindness. Thus: "Mr. Smith, may I introduce Mr. Jones? Mr. Jones has just returned from South America, where he has been inspecting a mine." I leave out, reluctantly, any discussion of the probability that Mr. Jones' statement about inspecting a mine was just a cock-and-bull story he told his wife when he packed up to go to South America. (I still think it was a cock-and-bull story, though.) Let us suppose that I am the Mr. Smith who has just been introduced to this Mr. Jones. Well, I would be more embarrassed by the introduction than helped. I know absolutely nothing about mines and almost as little about South America. Naturally, after Mrs. Barker's introduction, Mr. Jones would expect me to say something to him about his mine. I can see him standing there, waiting. And I know just how the talk would go for the first few minutes. "Well," I would say, and stop. Then: "How is the mine?" Mr. Jones would raise his eyebrows slightly and say, stiffly, "I beg your pardon?" I would then (sparring for time) wipe my shoes with a handkerchief, look up, find his eyes still on me, and say, "I mean—is the mine all right?" Mr. Jones would be certain to read into this some veiled aspersion on his mine (particulary if it was a woman, and not a mine, that he had down there), and in a short while we would be enemies for life. That would be all right with me, too, because I have enough friends the way it is, but I am thinking of the young Newark engineers who haven't any friends.

I kept trying to remember, in reading Barker on Behavior, that it was originally written for these young Newark engineers and not for me. But even so, I am not sure that it was fitting or fair for her to tell them that "the girl who is a total loss in a ballroom may have a good many attractive girl friends to whom she would gladly introduce you, and furthermore, she may be a real person whom you would like to know outside the ballroom." Now, I don't set myself up as the greatest authority in the world on this subject, but I have known a great many total losses in my day, and I can say in all fairness and calmness that not one of them ever brought up a lot of attractive girl friends whom she was glad to introduce me to. I don't believe that any total loss in the country has a lot of attractive girl friends or, if she has, that she would be eager to introduce you to them. Moreover, I never knew a total loss who proved to be a real person whom I liked very much to know outside the ballroom. I'll admit that I never saw any of these losses outside the first ballroom in which I met them, but a man of the world does not have to go through every experience to know what it is like. Furthermore, I have compared notes with other men of the world. They all say the same thing.

Mrs. Barker takes up a lot of other topics which I should like to go into, but I have neither the time nor the tolerance for all of them. I do, however, feel impelled to discuss her rule No. 1 under "A Few Rules to be Remembered in Your Association with Women." This rule is: "Ladies always go first except going upstairs, or in a possibly dangerous place. The gentleman goes ahead to help her into a boat, up a slippery incline, or up a ladder." That may be a good rule for the stronger and more agile young engineers, but it is hardly a rule which may be applied, as Mrs. Barker applies it here, to all gentlemen, including the sedentary and the nearsighted. In my own case, I can think of no woman friend of mine who would dream of letting me step into a canoe and then try to hand her into it. Most of my women friends would be perfectly willing—and eager—to get into the canoe first, rules or no rules, and then help me in—with the aid of their husbands, a couple of ropes, and a board. My difficulties with watercraft began some fifteen years ago at Green Lake, New York, when in stepping into a canoe I accidentally trod on a sleeping Boston terrier that I didn't know was in the canoe. I had a firm hold on a young woman's hand at the time, since I was about to assist her into the canoe (I was a stickler for rules in my youth). What followed was a deplorable and improbable fiasco, but it followed. The woman I was assisting at the time and the women she has talked to about the happenings of that day—in other words, all my other women friends —would rather stay behind and burn up than follow me up a ladder. And as for a slippery incline, nobody who saw me try to recover a woman's English sheep-dog puppy for her one icy day two years ago in Sixth Avenue at Fourteenth Street— the dog had slipped its leash—would want to follow me up a slippery incline. That goes for the dog, too.

10. Remembrance of Things Past

I READ THE OTHER DAY ABOUT SOME CHICKENS THAT GOT DRUNK on mash; out in Iowa, I believe it was. I was reminded of the last chickens that I got drunk. They belonged to a French woman who owned a farm in Normandy, near Granville, where I stayed from early spring until late autumn, ten years ago. The drunken chickens make as good a point of beginning as any for my recollections of Madame Goriaut, who owned the farm. I feel that I owe her some small memoir.

I recall the little farmhouse clearly. I saw it first in a slanting rain, as I walked past sheep meadows in which poppies were blooming. A garrulous, tall old man with a blowing white beard walked with me to the farm. He dealt in clocks and watches and real estate, and it was in his dim, ticking shop in the village of Cassis that I had heard of Madame Goriaut's and the room on the second floor which she rented out when she could. I think he went along to be sure that he would get his commission for directing me there.

The room was long and high and musty, with a big, soft bed, and windows that looked out on the courtyard of the place. It was like a courtyard, anyway, in form and in feeling. It should have held old wagon wheels and busy men in leather aprons, but the activity I remember was that of several black-and-white kittens stalking each other in a circular bed of red geraniums, which, of course, is not like a courtyard, but never-theless I remember the space in front of the house as being like a courtyard. A courtyard, let us say, with black-and-white kittens stalking each other in a circular bed of red geraniums.

The kittens were wild and unapproachable. Perhaps the fear of man had been struck into their hearts by Madame Goriaut. She was a formidable woman, almost, in a way, *épouvantable* (*épouvantable* was her favorite word—every-thing was *épouvantable*: the miserable straw crop, the storms off the Channel, the state of the nation, America's delay in

getting into the war). Madame was large and shapeless and possessed of an unforgettable toothiness. Her smile, under her considerable mustache, was quick and savage and frightening, like a flash of lightning lighting up a ruined woods. Whether she was tremendously amused (as by the fidgetings of a hang-ing rabbit—they hang rabbits for the table in Normandy) or tremendously angry (as over the breaking of a crock by her sulky little daughter) you could not determine by her expres-sion. She raised her upper lip and showed her teeth and bel-lowed, in anger as well as in gaiety. You could identify her moods only by her roaring words, which reverberated around the house like the reports of shotguns. There was no midpoint in her spirit: she was either greatly pleased, usually about nothing much, or greatly displeased, by very little more.

Like many French people in the provinces, Madame Goriaut believed that all Americans were rich. She would ask me if I had not paid a thousand francs for my shoes. My spectacle rims were of solid gold, to be sure. I carried—was it not so? —a thousand dollars in my pockets for tobacco and odds and ends. I would turn my pockets inside out to show her this was not true. At these times she frightened me. It was not too fantastic to conceive of Madame Goriaut creeping into one's room at night with a kitchen knife and a basket, come to pluck one's thousand dollars and one's life as she might pluck spinach. I was always slightly alarmed by her. She had but little English—"I love you," "kiss me," "thousand dollars," "no," and "yes." I don't know where she learned these words, but she enjoyed repeating them, in that order, and with heavy delight, like a child who has learned a poem. Sometimes she gave me the shudders saying, apropos of nothing at all, "I love you, kiss me, thousand dollars, no, yes."

Madame Goriaut was a widow. Her husband had been a great professor, she told me. He had died a few years before, leaving her the farm, no money, and two five-act plays in blank verse. She showed the plays to me the first day I was there. They were written in ink in a fine hand. I picked them up and put them down with an imitation of awed pleasure. I wondered what her husband could have been like, the great professor. I found out a little now and then. Once I asked her if she had a photograph of him and she said no, because he had believed that in the transference of one's image to a film or plate there departed a certain measure of one's substance. Did I believe this was true? I said I did indeed. I was afraid to refute any of the convictions of the great professor when Madame put them to me with her leer and her fierce, sudden laugh. Of these convictions the only other I remember is that M. Goriaut believed he would come back after death as a *hirondelle,* or swallow. There were a lot of swallows around the farmhouse and the barns, and Madame Goriaut asked me if I thought that one of them was her husband. I asked her, in turn, if any of the swallows had ever made her a sign. She bellowed with laughter. I couldn't tell much about that laugh. I couldn't tell what she had thought of her husband alive, or what she believed of him dead.

I got the chickens drunk one Sunday morning by throwing to them pieces of bread soaked in Calvados, strong, new Calvados. Madame had invaded my room one Saturday night after dinner to ask me again why America had got into the war so late. She was bitter on that subject. While she talked she noticed that I had a bottle of Bénédictine on my desk. She said that Bénédictine was not the thing; I must have Calvados, the grand *eau de vie* of the region; she would give me a bottle of it. She went downstairs and brought it up to me, a large bottle. *"Voilà!"* she roared, planking it down on the table. I thanked her. Later she charged me seven francs for it on my weekly bill. I couldn't drink the stuff, it was so green and violent, so I fed it to the chickens. They got very drunk and fell down and got up and fell down again. Madame did not know what was the matter, and she raged around the village about a new disease that had come to kill the chickens and to impoverish her. The chickens were all right by Monday morning—that is, physically. Mentally, I suppose, it was their worst day.

Once I went with Madame Goriaut and her daughter, who was about seven but was peaked and whiny and looked twelve, to a village fair in Cassis. The little girl led the family donkey by his halter. It turned out when we got there that they were going to offer the donkey for sale; it seems that they offered him for sale every year at the fair. Madame hung a little sign around his neck saying that he was for sale; she had carried the sign to the fair wrapped in a newspaper. Nobody bought the donkey, but one man stepped up and asked how old he was. The little girl replied, "Twelve years!" Madame Goriaut flew into one of her rages and cuffed the child to the ground with the back of her hand. "But he has only eight years, Monsieur!" she bellowed at the man, who was moving away. She followed him, bellowing, but he evaded her and she returned, still bellowing. She told me later that the donkey was twenty-four years old. Her daughter, she said, would make some man a miserable wife one day.

After the fair we went to a three-table *terrasse* on a narrow sidewalk in front of a tawdy café in the village and she ordered Calvados. There was, I noticed, a small insect in my glass when it was set in front of me. I called to the waiter, but he had gone back into the café and didn't hear me. Madame asked what was the matter, and I showed her the insect in the bottom of the glass. She shrugged, said *"Ah, làl,"* and exchanged glasses with me. She drank the insect placidly. When I paid for the drinks, I brought out a new five-franc note. The little girl's eyes widened and she grabbed for it. *"Quel joli billet de cinq francs!"* she squealed. Her mother slapped her down again, shouting that the *joli billet* belonged to Monsieur, who was a wealthy gentleman unused to *épouvantables* children. The little girl cried sullenly. *"Par exemple!"* cried Madame, with her toothy leer. "But you may make her a small present when you leave us." We had another drink against the black day when I should leave them.

The day I left a man came for me and my bags in a two-wheeled cart. It was getting on toward November and Normandy had grown chill. A cold rain was falling. I piled my bags in the back of the cart and was about to shake hands with Madame when the little girl squealed that I had not given her the present I had promised her. I took a five-franc note from my billfold and handed it to her. She grabbed it and ran, screaming in delight, a delight that turned to terror as Madame, bellowing her loudest, set off in pursuit. They disappeared around a corner of the house, and I could hear them screaming and bellowing in the orchard behind the house. I climbed into the cart and told the man to drive on. He said it was always like that with the young ones nowadays, they wanted everything for themselves. I was gone long before Madame came back, as I suppose she did, to say goodbye. I couldn't have faced her. I sometimes wonder about the little girl. She must be seventeen by now, and is probably already making some man a miserable wife.

11. *Something About Polk*

H URRYING TOWARD SHILOH THROUGH THE PAGES OF MR. W. E. Woodward's "Meet General Grant," a book published nine years ago, which I only recently came upon—in the library of a summer hotel—I ran into a provocative marginal note, indignantly written with pencil, on page 73. In the middle of that page occurs this sentence by Mr. Woodward: "James K. Polk, an insignificant Tennessee politician, who was almost unknown to the American people, was nominated by the Democrats . . ." The pencilled note in the margin opposite this said sharply, "Governor of Tennessee. Twice Speaker of the House of Representatives. The Jackson leader in the fight against the U. S. Bank. Almost unknown?"

I left General Grant and Mr. Woodward to shift for themselves, and gave myself up to quiet contemplation of this astonishing note. Here was the bold imprint of a person who, eighty or more years after Polk's death, could actually give three facts about the man. I was moved to wonder and a kind of admiration for this last of the Polk men, rising up so unexpectedly out of that margin, shaking a white, tense fist, defending his hero. For of all our array of Presidents, there was none less memorable than James K. Polk. If ten patriots, picked at random, were asked to list the names of all the Presidents, it is likely that most of them would leave out the name of the eleventh. Even if they remembered his name, surely none of them could put down a fact about him. He was a man of

141

no arresting achievement. The achievements that our mysterious marginal apologist puts down are certainly not the kind of achievements that make a man well known. Who knows the name of the present Governor of Tennessee? How many people know the name of the Speaker of the House? (Did I hear somebody say Joe Cannon?)

There are a number of other Presidents whom the average patriot, in making a list, might leave out, but in his day each of these others was notable for something unusual, no matter how minor. Pierce was thrown from his horse in the Mexican War, wearing the uniform of a brigadier general; he was the youngest man to be elected to the Presidency up to that time. Andrew Johnson's wife taught him to write; he was said to have been cockeyed one day when, as Vice-President, he addressed the Senate; he was the only President who was ever impeached. Buchanan was the only bachelor President. Tyler served eggnogs and mint juleps in the White House. The first Harrison died in office. And so it goes, the enlivening story of all the Presidents except Polk. It is unquestionably true that he was almost unknown to the American people when he was elected. They never got to know him well; after his term was over, he retired to his home and died there three months later.

The trouble with Polk was that he never did anything to catch the people's eye; he never gave them anything to remember him by; nothing happened to him. He never cut down a cherry tree, he didn't tell funny stories, he was not impeached, he was not shot, he didn't drink heavily, he didn't gamble, he wasn't involved in scandal. He was a war President, to be sure, but his activities in the White House during the Mexican War were overshadowed by the activities in the field of an old buzzard named Zachary Taylor, whose soldiers called him "Old Rough and Ready." Polk never had a nickname; it is likely that he was James to his friends, not Jim. His closest friend—his Farley, his Harry Daugherty—was a man you have never heard of. His name was Gideon J. Pillow.

James K. Polk seemed destined to be overshadowed by other men. He was once even overshadowed by a mythical man, and many who have forgotten the name of Polk will remember the name of the mythical man. In 1844 the Whigs circulated the story that Polk had once taken a gang of Negroes to the South to be sold, each one branded "J.K.P." When asked where they got this infamous story, the Whigs said they had read it in an authoritative travel book written by one Baron Von Roorback. There was no such man, but the word "roorback," meaning a last-minute political trick, has gone into the American language. And the real man the mythical man wrote about has been forgotten. I encountered the Roorback story in Carl Sandburg's "Abraham Lincoln: The Prairie Years," in which I also found an anecdote about Mrs. Polk, but none about Mr. Polk. Thus he was even overshadowed by his wife. It seems that at a reception following Polk's inaugural, someone said to Mrs. Polk, "Madam, you have a very genteel assemblage tonight." to which Mrs. Polk replied, "Sir, I have never seen it otherwise." It wasn't very much, to be sure, but it was something; it has lived a hundred years. The President himself that night does not appear to have opened his trap.

One begins to feel sorry for poor Mr. Polk and the oblivion that has fallen upon him. Here is a President of the United States unremembered for any deed, unremembered even for any anecdote. I am for the formation of a Society for the Invention of Amusing Anecdotes about James K. Polk. I am willing to suggest a few myself to get the thing started. In fifty or a hundred years these anecdotes will begin to appear in histories and biographies. The forgotten President deserves a break; after all, he was a splendid gentleman. Let us see what we can do for James K. Polk, whom Abraham Lincoln once called a "bewildered, confounded, miserably perplexed man."

We might begin with that crack of Lincoln's. Old Gideon Pillow, let us say, came to Polk one day and told him that Abe Lincoln had said he was "bewildered, confounded, and miserably perplexed." "You tell Lincoln," said Polk, "that I've never been so bewildered I couldn't tell the back of a shovel from a piece of writing paper." A little cruel, to be sure, but then Lincoln had asked for it; at least we are showing that our man had spirit. He also had a nice whimsey. A Democrat office-seeker once stormed into his office (we will say) and confronted the President. "First they tell me to see Gideon Pillow and then they tell me to see you," said the man. "I don't know *where* to go." "Ah," said the President, "shunted from Pillow to Polk." Not one of the great puns, perhaps, but it shows our man was human and quick on the uptake. Personally, I think everybody is going to like this next anecdote, about Polk and General Zachary Taylor (that's what we need, anecdotes of the Lincoln-Grant variety). It seems that an indignant Whig came to Polk one day and told him that General Taylor was drinking too much. "He has to," said Polk. "If he didn't see twice as many of those cowardly Mexicans as there really are, he wouldn't have the heart to fight them." The Whig visitor was outraged. "Do you mean to say that you recommend drinking?" he demanded. "Not for myself, if that's what you mean," said Polk. "You see, what *I* have to look at is Whigs."

These are all that I can think of myself, and I am afraid that none of them is going to hurl our hero into immortality, but at least they are a start in the right direction. Let somebody else try it. There's no great rush.

12. *Aisle Seats in the Mind*

I FOLLOW AS CLOSELY AS ANYONE, PROBABLY MORE CLOSELY THAN most people, the pronouncements on life, death, and the future of the movies as given out from time to time by Miss Mary Pickford. Some friends of mine think that it has even become a kind of obsession with me. I wouldn't go so far as to say that, but I do admit that many times when I would ordinarily sit back and drink my brandy and smoke a cigar and become a little drowsy mentally and a little sodden intellectually, something that Mary Pickford has just said engages my inner attention so that instead of dozing off, I am kept as bright-eyed and alert as a hunted deer. Often I wake up at night, too, and lie there thinking about life, and death, and the future of the movies. Miss Pickford's latest arresting observation came in an interview with a *World-Telegram* correspondent out in Beverly Hills. Said Miss Pickford, in part, "Any type of salaciousness is as distasteful to Mr. Lasky as it is to me. There will be no salaciousness at all in our films. Not one little bit! We will consider only those stories which will insure wholesome, healthy, yet vital entertainment. *Be a guardian, not an usher, at the portal of your thought.*"

Miss Pickford has a way which I can only call intriguing, much as I hate the word, of throwing out little rounded maxims, warnings, and morals at the ends of her paragraphs. I had a great-aunt who did the same thing, and in my teens she fascinated and frightened me; perhaps that is why Miss Pickford's exhortations so engross me, and keep me from the dicing tables, the dens of vice, and the more salacious movies, poems, and novels. Miss Pickford's newest precept has occupied a great many of my waking hours since I read it, and quite a few of my sleeping ones. In the first place, it has brought me sharply up against the realization that I am not a guardian at the portal of my thought and that, what is more, being now

A Trio of Thoughts

forty-two years of age, I probably never will be. What I am like at the portal of my thought is one of those six-foot-six ushers who used to stand around the lobby of the Hippodrome during performances of "Jumbo." (They were not really ushers, but doormen, I think, but let us consider them as ushers for the sake of the argument.) What I want to convey is that I am *all* usher, as far as the portal of my thought goes, terribly usher. But I am unlike the "Jumbo" ushers or any other ushers in that I show any and all thoughts to their seats whether they have tickets or not. They can be under-age and without their parents, or they can be completely cockeyed,

or they can show up without a stitch on; I let them in and
show them to the best seats in my mind (the ones in the
royal arena and the gold boxes).

I don't want you to think that all I do is let in *salacious*
thoughts. Salacious thoughts can get in along with any others,
including those that are under-age and those that are cockeyed,
but my mental audience is largely made up of thoughts that
are, I am sorry to say, idiotic. For days a thought has been
running around in the aisles of my mind, singing and shouting, a thought that, if I were a guardian, I would certainly
have barred at the portal or thrown out instantly as soon
as it got in. This thought is one without reason or motivation,
but it keeps singing, over and over, to a certain part of the
tune of "For He's a Jolly Good Fellow," these words:

> A message for Captain Bligh,
> And a greeting to Franchot Tone.

I hope it doesn't slip by the guardian at your own portal of
thought, but, whether it does or not, it is sung to that part of
the aforementioned tune the words of which go "Which nobody can deny, which nobody can deny." And it is pretty
easy, if you are the usher type, to let it into your mind, where
it is likely to get all your other thoughts to singing the same
thing, just as Donald Duck did to the orchestra in "The Band
Concert." Where it came from I don't know. Thoughts like
that can spot the usher type of mind a mile away, and they
seek it out as tramps seek out the backdoors of generous
farm wives.

Just last Sunday another vagrant thought came up to the
portal of my mind, or, rather, was shown up to the portal of
my mind, and I led it instantly to a seat down front, where
much to my relief, it has been shouting even more loudly
than the Captain Bligh-Franchot Tone thought and is, in fact,

about to cause that thought to leave the theatre. This new thought was introduced at my portal by my colored maid, Margaret, who, in seeking to describe a certain part of the electric refrigerator which she said was giving trouble, called it "doom-shaped." Since Margaret pronounced that wonderful word, everything in my mind and everything in the outside world has taken on the shape of doom. If I were a true guardian of the portal of my thought, I would have refused that expression admittance, because it is too provocative, too edgy, and too dark, for comfort, but then I would have missed the unique and remarkable experience that I had last Sunday, when, just as night was falling, I walked down a doom-shaped street under a doom-shaped sky and up a doom-shaped staircase to my doom-shaped apartment. Like Miss Pickford, I am all for the wholesome, the healthy, and the vital, but sometimes I think one's mind can become, if one is the guardian type, too wholesome, healthy, and vital to be much fun. Any mind, I say boldly here and now, which would not let a doom-shaped thought come in and take a seat is not a mind that I want around.

As in all my discourses about Miss Pickford and her philosophy, I am afraid I have drifted ever so slightly from the main point, which, in this case, I suppose, is the question of keeping salacious thoughts out of the mind, and not doom-shaped ones, or Franchot Tone. Miss Pickford, however, is to blame for my inability to stick to the exact point, because of her way of following up some specific thought, such as the unanimity of her and Mr. Lasky's feelings about salaciousness, with an extremely challenging and all-encompassing injunction, such as that everybody should be a guardian at the portal of his thought, and not an usher.

I have brooded for a long time about the origin of Miss Pickford's injunction. I am not saying that she did not think it up herself. It's hers and she's welcome to it, as far as I am concerned (I'd rather have "doom-shaped" for my own). But I somehow feel that she was quoting someone and that the only reason she didn't add "as the poet has it" or "as the fella said" is that she naturally supposes that everybody would know who wrote the line. I don't happen to know; I don't happen ever to have heard it before. It may be that it is a product of one of the immortal minds, but somehow I doubt that. To me it sounds like Eddie Guest or the late Ella Wheeler Wilcox. It may have been tossed off, of course, in a bad moment, by John Cowper Powys, or Gene Tunney, or Senator Victor Donahey of Ohio, but I am inclined to think not. If you should happen to know, for certain, that it is the work of Shakespeare or Milton, there is no use in your calling me up about it, or sending a telegram. By the time I could hear from you, I would have got it out of my mind, and only "doom-shaped" would be there, sitting in a darkened theatre. I would like that, so please let us alone.

13. Suli Suli

I ALWAYS TRY TO ANSWER ABERCROMBIE & FITCH'S QUESTIONS (in their advertisements) the way they obviously want them answered, but usually, if I am to be honest with them and with myself, I must answer them in a way that would not please Abercrombie & Fitch. While that company and I have always nodded and smiled pleasantly enough when we met, we have never really been on intimate terms, mainly because we have so little in common. For one thing, I am inclined to be nervous and impatient, whereas Abercrombie & Fitch are at all times composed and tranquil. In the case of a man and a woman this disparity in temperament sometimes works out all right, but with Abercrombie & Fitch and me it is different: neither one of us is willing to submerge any part of his personality in the other, or compromise in matters of precedent, habit, or tradition. Yet in spite of all the natural barriers between Abercrombie & Fitch and myself, we are drawn to each other by a curious kind of fascination, or perhaps it is only me who is drawn to them. Not long ago I dropped in at their store to browse around among all the glittering objects, when suddenly I was faced by a tall and courteous but firm clerk who asked me if there was anything he could do for me. I said instantly, "I want to buy a javelin."

Now, it is true that I have always wanted to buy a javelin, because I have always wanted to see how far I could throw one, but two things had, up to the day I am telling about, kept me from going ahead with the thing. First, I had been

afraid that I would not be able to throw a javelin as far as
Babe Didrikson used to throw one, and I knew that the dis-
covery that a woman could throw anything farther than I
could throw it would have a depressing effect on me and
might show up in my work and in my relationships with
women. Second, I did not know how Abercrombie & Fitch,
of whom I have ever been slightly in awe, would take my
wanting to buy a javelin. They are, to be sure, a very courteous firm, but they have a way of looking at you sometimes as

if you had left your spoon in your coffee cup. However, all
my fears and uncertainties were beside the point, because here
I was, finally asking Abercrombie & Fitch for a javelin.

"A *javelin*?" said Abercrombie & Fitch (I shall call the
clerk that), and I knew instantly from his inflection that he
did not think I should have a javelin and, furthermore, I
knew that I was not going to get one. Somehow or other it
was not the thing for a tall, thin man in a blue suit to come
in and ask for a javelin. I was, naturally, embarrassed. "I—
uh—yes, I had thought some of purchasing a javelin," I said.
"It's for a rather—a sort of special use, in a way, I mean, what
I want, of course, is *two* javelins; that is, a *pair* of javelins, so
that I could cross them, like oars, you know, or guns, above
a mantelpiece. I have oars and guns, of course, but I—I—"
Beyond this I could not go with a story that was becoming
more and more difficult for me and, I daresay, stranger and

stranger to Abercrombie & Fitch. A kind of feverish high note was in my voice, a note that always betrays me when I am lying. "I am very sorry," said Abercrombie & Fitch, his eyebrows raised slightly, "but we have no javelins in stock." He paused; then, "I could order one for you." He knew, you see, that I really only wanted one; my story about wanting two had not fooled him for a minute. I think he also suspected that I wanted to find out whether I could throw the thing as far as Babe Didrikson. Abercrombie & Fitch can read me like a book; I don't know just why. I told the clerk to let it go, not to bother, and to cover my confusion I bought a set of lawn bowls, although I have no lawn that I could possibly use for bowls. I believe the clerk knew that, too.

But I am straying from the point I began with, about Abercrombie & Fitch's questions, the ones I can almost never answer the way they would like to have them answered. Take the one recently printed in an advertisement in the *New Yorker*. Under a picture of a man fishing in a stream were these words: "Can't you picture yourself in the middle of the stream with the certain knowledge that a wise old trout is hiding under a ledge and defying you to tempt him with your skillfully cast fly?" My answer, of course, is "No." Especially if I am to be equipped the way the gentleman in the illustration is equipped: with rod, reel, line, net, hip boots, felt hat, and pipe. They might just as well add a banjo and a parachute to my equipment, along with a grandfather's clock, for with anything at all to handle in the middle of a rushing brook I would drown faster than you could say "J. Robins." The wise old trout would have the laugh of his life, especially when I begin to cast. I tried casting in a stream only twice, and the first time I caught a tree and the second time I barely missed landing one of a group of picnickers. Therefore, I cannot agree with Abercrombie & Fitch's ad when it says further: "Words are poor to express the delight of just handling a beautiful rod with a sweet-singing reel and a line that seems alive as it answers the flick of your wrist." It seems alive all right, but it answers different men in different ways; with me, it is surly to the point of impudence. No, I am afraid I am not going to send for one of the fly-fishing catalogues the company advertised or drop in and look at their "complete trout outfits." Abercrombie & Fitch would know, just glancing at me, that I would be at the mercy of the complete trout outfit, and of the trout, too—if they were brave enough to come at me when I went down in a tangle of rod, reel, line, net, boots, pipe, and hat.

I am sorry to have to say this to Abercrombie & Fitch, but fishing of any kind is something I don't like to picture myself doing. Oh, I've tried fishing of various kinds, but I never seemed to get the hang of any of them. I still remember a gay fishing party I went on with a lot of strong men and beautiful girls, when I was still fairly strong myself. It was a fine day and it was a pleasant creek and the fish were biting. Everybody except me was pulling in perch and pickerel, or whatever they were—all fish look exactly alike to me. I kept pulling out of the water an aged and irritable turtle. No matter where I moved along the bank or where I dropped my line, I would hook the turtle. Nobody else got him, but I got him variously, by the leg, the back of his shell, and his belly, but never securely; he wouldn't swallow the hook, he just monkeyed with it. He would always drop back into the water as I was about to haul him in. I didn't really want him, but I wanted to get him out of the way. It furnished a great deal of amusement for everybody, except me and the turtle. Another time I went fishing on Lake Skaneateles with a group of people, including a lovely young woman named Sylvia. On this occasion I actually did hook a fish, even before anybody else had a bite, and I brought it into the rowboat with a great plop. Then, not having had any experience with a caught fish, I didn't know what to do with it. I had had some vague idea that a fish died quietly and with dignity as soon as it was flopped into a boat, but that, of course, was an erroneous idea. It leaped about strenuously. I got pretty far away from it and stared at it. The young lady named Sylvia finally grabbed it expertly and slapped it into insensibility against the sides and bottom of the boat. I think it was perhaps then that I decided to go in for javelin-throwing and began to live with the dream of being able to throw a javelin farther than Babe Didrikson. A man never completely gets over the chagrin and shock of having a woman handle for him the fish he has caught.

As for deep-sea fishing, you and I—and Abercrombie & Fitch—know that an old turtle-catcher is not going to be able to cope with a big-game fish that fights you for ten or twelve hours and drags you from Miami to Jacksonville. Every time I read an article about deep-sea fishing I realize more thoroughly than ever that, as far as I am concerned, all the sailfish and tuna and tarpon are as safe as if they were in bank vaults. In a recent piece in *Esquire,* Mr. Hemingway tells about a man who hooked an eighty-pound fish which, before the man could pull it in, was grabbed up far below the surface by some unknown monster of the deep, who took a bite at it and let it go. When the original quarry was brought up, it was seen that the other fish had "squeezed it and held it so that every bit of the insides of the fish had been crushed out while the huge fish moved off with the eighty-pound fish in its mouth." "What size of a fish would that be?" Mr. Hemingway asks. He needn't look at me. I do not stick in boats very well, particularly if they are being jerked around by a fish that has another fish in its mouth, and I never expect to get near enough to their habitat to make even a wild guess as to their size.

Then there was an article I came on in, of all magazines, the *East African Annual,* for 1934-35, called "Sea Fishing Off the Coast of Kenya," by Mr. Hugh Copley. In Africa, you can get big, strong black natives (Suli Suli they are called, I think) to go out in a boat with you, but I am afraid they would only hamper and confuse me. Mr. Copley lists the names of the big fish you can pursue along the Kenya coast, giving first the English name, then the technical name, and then the native, or Swahili, name. The list begins this way: "1. The sailfish (Istiophorus gladius), Suli Suli. 2. Herschel's spearfish (Makaira herscheli), Suli Suli." The predicaments that an American, and I mean me, might get into deep-sea fishing with a native that called everything Suli Suli are infinite. I don't even like to think about it. Nor would I ever be able to look after my tackle the way Mr. Copley says it should be looked after, because I would never get anything else done except that, day in and day out. He writes, "Lines must be dried every evening. Reels taken apart and greased. When the fishing trip is over soak all the lines for a night in fresh water and they dry thoroughly for a whole day. All hooks, wire traces, must be greased; gaffs cleaned with emery paper and then greased. The rod should be examined for broken whippings; these replaced and the rod given three coats of best coach varnish." I have a pretty vivid picture of what I would look like after all that greasing and regreasing. And then, of course, the whole thing falls down for me when it comes to the three coats that have to be put on the rod. I might go into Abercrombie & Fitch and ask for a javelin, as indeed I did, but I would never think of going up to one of their clerks and saying, "I should like to buy a bottle of coach varnish." I have no idea what would happen, but the episode would be, I am sure, most unfortunate.

14. An Outline of Scientists

HAVING BEEN LAID UP BY A BUMBLEBEE FOR A COUPLE OF weeks, I ran through the few old novels there were in the cottage I had rented in Bermuda and finally was reduced to reading "The Outline of Science, a Plain Story Simply Told," in four volumes. These books were published by Putnam's fifteen years ago and were edited by J. Arthur Thomson, Regius Professor of Natural History at the University of Aberdeen. The volumes contained hundreds of articles written by various scientists and over eight hundred illustrations, forty of which, the editor bragged on the flyleaf, were in color. A plain story simply told with a lot of illustrations, many of them in color, seemed just about the right mental fare for a man who had been laid up by a bee. Human nature being what it is, I suppose the morbid reader is more interested in how I happened to be laid up by a bee than in what I found in my scientific research, so I will dismiss that unfortunate matter in a few words. The bee stung me in the foot and I got an infection (staphylococcus, for short). It was the first time in my life that anything smaller than a turtle had ever got the best of me, and naturally I don't like to dwell on it. I prefer to go on to my studies in "The Outline of Science," if everybody is satisfied.

I happened to pick up Volume IV first and was presently in the midst of a plain and simple explanation of the Einstein theory, a theory about which in my time I have done as much talking as the next man, although I admit now that I never understood it very clearly. I understood it even less clearly after I had tackled a little problem about a man running a hundred-yard dash and an aviator in a plane above him. Everything, from the roundness of the earth to the immortality of the soul, has been demonstrated by the figures of men in action, but here was a new proposition. It seems that if the aviator were travelling as fast as light, the stop watch held by the track

judge would not, from the aviator's viewpoint, move at all. (You've got to make believe that the aviator could see the watch, which is going to be just as hard for you as it was for me.) You might think that this phenomenon of the unmoving watch hand would enable the runner to make a hundred yards in nothing flat, but, if so, you are living in a fool's paradise. To an aviator going as fast as light, the hundred-yard track would shrink to nothing at all. If the aviator were going *twice* as fast as light, the report of the track judge's gun would wake up the track judge, who would still be in bed in his pajamas, not yet having got up to go to the track meet. This last is my own private extension of the general theory, but it seems to me as sound as the rest of it.

I finally gave up the stop watch and the airplane, and went deeper into the chapter till I came to the author's summary of a scientific romance called "Lumen," by the celebrated French astronomer, M. Flammarion (in my youth, the Hearst Sunday feature sections leaned heavily on M. Flammarion's discoveries). The great man's lurid little romance deals, it seems, with a man who died in 1864 and whose soul flew with the speed of thought to one of the stars in the constellation Capella. This star was so far from the earth that it took light rays seventy-two years to get there, hence the man's soul kept catching up with light rays from old historical events and passing them. Thus the man's soul was able to see the battle of Waterloo, fought backward. First the man's soul—oh, let's call him Mr. Lumen—first Mr. Lumen saw a lot of dead soldiers and then he saw them get up and start fighting. "Two hundred thousand corpses, come to life, marched off the field in perfect order," wrote M. Flammarion. Perfect order, I should think, only backward.

I kept going over and over this section of the chapter on the Einstein theory. I even tried reading it backward, twice as fast as light, to see if I could capture Napoleon at Waterloo while he was still home in bed. If you are interested in the profound mathematical theory of the distinguished German scientist, you may care to glance at a diagram I drew for my own guidance, as follows:

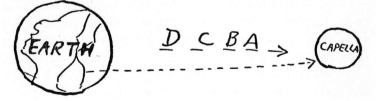

Now, A represents Napoleon entering the field at Waterloo and B represents his defeat there. The dotted line is, of course, Mr. Lumen, going hell-for-leather. C and D you need pay no particular attention to; the first represents the birth of Mr. George L. Snively, an obscure American engineer, in 1819, and the second the founding of the New England Glass Company, in 1826. I put them in to give the thing roundness and verisimilitude and to suggest that Mr. Lumen passed a lot of other events besides Waterloo.

In spite of my diagram and my careful reading and rereading of the chapter on the Einstein theory, I left it in the end with a feeling that my old grip on it, as weak as it may have been, was stronger than my new grip on it, and simpler, since it had not been mixed up with aviators, stop watches, Mr. Lumen, and Napoleon. The discouraging conviction crept over me that science was too much for me, that these brooding scientists, with their bewildering problems, many of which work backward, live on an intellectual level which I, who think of a hundred-yard dash as a hundred-dash, could never attain to. It was with relief that I drifted on to Chapter XXXVI, "The Story of Domesticated Animals." There wouldn't be anything in that going as fast as light or faster, and it was more the kind of thing that a man who has been put to bed by a bee should read for the alleviation of his humiliation. I picked out the section on dogs, and very shortly I came to this: "There are few dogs which do not inspire affection; many crave it. But there are some which seem to repel us, like the bloodhound. True, man has made him what he is. Terrible to look at and terrible to encounter, man has raised him up to hunt down his fellowman." Accompanying the article was a picture of a dignified and mournful-looking bloodhound, about as terrible to look at as Abraham Lincoln, about as terrible to encounter as Jimmy Durante.

Poor, frightened little scientist! I wondered who he was, this man whom Mr. J. Arthur Thomson, Regius Professor of Natural History at the University of Aberdeen, had selected to inform the world about dogs. Some of the chapters were signed, but this one wasn't, and neither was the one on the Einstein theory (you were given to understand that they had all been written by eminent scientists, however). I had the strange feeling that both of these articles had been written by the same man. I had the strange feeling that *all* scientists are the same man. Could it be possible that I had isolated here, as under a microscope, the true nature of the scientist? It pleased me to think so; it still pleases me to think so. I have never liked or trusted scientists very much, and I think now that I know why: they are afraid of bloodhounds. They must, therefore, be afraid of frogs, jack rabbits, and the larger pussy-cats. This must be the reason that most of them withdraw from the world and devote themselves to the study of the inanimate and the impalpable. Out of my analysis of those few sentences on the bloodhound, one of the gentlest of all breeds of dogs, I have arrived at what I call Thurber's Law, which is that scientists don't really know anything about anything. I doubt everything they have ever discovered. I don't think light has a speed of 7,000,000 miles per second at all (or whatever the legendary speed is). Scientists just think light is going that fast, because they are afraid of it. It's so terrible to look at. I have always suspected that light just plodded along, and now I am positive of it.

I can understand how that big baby dropped the subject of bloodhounds with those few shuddering sentences, but I propose to scare him and his fellow-scientists a little more about the huge and feral creatures. Bloodhounds are some-times put on the trail of old lost ladies or little children who have wandered away from home. When a bloodhound finds an old lady or a little child, he instantly swallows the old lady or the little child whole, clothes and all. This is probably what happened to Charlie Ross, Judge Crater, Agnes Tufverson, and a man named Colonel Appel, who disappeared at the battle of Shiloh. God only knows how many thousands of people bloodhounds have swallowed, but it is probably twice as many as the Saint Bernards have swallowed. As everybody knows, the Saint Bernards, when they find travellers fainting in the snow, finish them off. Monks have notoriously little to eat and it stands to reason they couldn't feed a lot of big, full-grown Saint Bernards; hence they sick them on the lost travellers, who would never get anywhere, anyway. The brandy in the little kegs the dogs wear around their necks is used by the Saint Bernards in drunken orgies that follow the killings.

I guess that's all I have to say to the scientists right now, except *boo!*

15. Highball Flags

IT IS A MATTER OF COMMON KNOWLEDGE AMONG SMART SEA-going gentlemen (if you keep your eyes open, you will have read about it) that the ubiquitous yachtsman can now purchase a cocktail flag for his pleasure craft. To quote an item I recently read on the subject, the flag has "a red glass on a white field" and it means "We're serving drinks." When it is flown upside down, it means "Who has a drink?" I know very little about the ways of yachtsmen but I have always thought of them as rather reserved, aristocratic gentlemen, not given to garrulity in flags, or to announcing private parties with flags, or to pub-lic—or rather high-seas—cadging of drinks with flags. Appar-ently I was wrong. The ancient practice of sailing a ship, once the prerogative of strong, silent men of retiring disposition, appears about to go the way the canoe went when the ukulele came along. The advent of the cocktail flag, with its strange device, seems likely to lead to a deplorable debasing of the dignity of yachts and yachting—and yachtsmen. Surely any-body will have to be allowed aboard who can climb aboard—that is, when the flag is flown right side up; and certainly all sorts of common and vulgar boats are going to come alongside, roaring and singing (and possibly carrying nothing but gin and ginger ale), when the flag is flown upside down. It is too late now to do anything about this except to suggest some further flag signals; as long as yachts are going in for open drinking and carousing, they may as well do the thing up right. No yachting party which has gone so far as to fly the cocktail flag upside down is going to be satisfied with that. There are a lot of other things the people on board will want to say, after they have run out of drinks and are bawling for more, and an array of signals for these other things might just as well be arranged now. I have a few suggestions to make

"Honey, Honey, Bless Your Heart"

along this line; yachtsmen can take them or they can let them alone. What I propose is a series of highball flags, to be run up after the cocktail flag has been struck.

Flag No. 1: The head of a woman, blue, on a white field. This means "My wife is the finest little girl in all the world."

Flag No. 2: Steel-colored fist on a crimson field. This means "I can lick any other yachtsman within sight of this flag." If flown upside down, this means the same thing plus "with one hand tied behind me."

Flag No. 3: Six gray fists rampant on a dark-blue field. This means "Let's all go over and beat hell out of the Monarch of

Bermuda" (or whatever other large, peaceful ship is lying nearest the yacht and the other yachts it is talking to).

Flag No. 4: White zigzag lightning flash on black field. This means "Let's have one more quick one and then we'll get the hell out of here."

Flag No. 5: Large scarlet question mark on white field. This means "Has anybody got a tenor on board?"

Flag No. 6: Red eye and pendent pear-shaped silver tear on black field. This means "You're bes' frien' ev' had." If hung upside down, it means "You're fines' ship ev' seen."

Flag No. 7: White stocking on scarlet field. This means "We want women!"

Flag No. 8: Black zigzag lightning flash on white field. This means the same as No. 4.

Flag No. 9: Four male heads, white eyes, red, open mouths, on smoky-gray field. This means, if right side up, "Let's sing 'Honey, Honey, Bless Your Heart'"; if upside down, "Let's sing 'I had a Dream, Dear.'" There should be one hundred other similar flags for the one hundred other songs men sing when in their cups, and also, of course, a black flag with a white thumb centered; when hung with the thumb pointing up, this means "O. K., you pitch it"; when hung with the thumb pointing down, it means "No, not 'Sweet Adeline'!"

Flag No. 111: Horizontal white line on sable field. This means "I got to lie down."

Flag No. 112: A large plain yellow flag. This means "I said I got to lie *down*!"

If you have any other ideas, don't send them to me, for my yellow flag is flying, upside down (which means "Gone to bed"); send them to Abercrombie & Fitch. They are selling the cocktail flags, or anyway they have them in stock.

16. Mrs. Phelps

WHEN I WENT TO COLUMBUS, OHIO, ON A VISIT RECENTLY, I
called one afternoon on Mrs. Jessie Norton, an old
friend of my mother's. Mrs. Norton is in her seventies, but
she is in bright possession of all her faculties (except that she
does not see very well without her spectacles and is forever
mislaying them). She always has a story to tell me over the
teacups. She reads my fortune in the tea leaves, too, before I
go, and for twenty years has told me that a slim, blonde
woman is going to come into my life and that I should beware
of the sea. Strange things happen to Mrs. Norton. She is
psychic. My mother once told me that Mrs. Norton had been
psychic since she was seven years old. Voices speak to her
in the night, cryptically, persons long dead appear to her in
dreams, and even her waking hours are sometimes filled
with a mystic confusion.

Mrs. Norton's story this time dealt with a singular experience she had had only a few months before. It seems that she
had gone to bed late on a blowy night, the kind of night on
which the wind moans in the wires, and telephone bells
ring without benefit of human agency, and there are inexplicable sounds at doors and windows. She had felt, as she got
into bed, that something was going to happen. Mrs. Norton
has never in her life had the feeling that something was going
to happen that something hasn't happened. Once it was the
Columbus flood, another time it was the shooting of McKinley,

still another time the disappearance forever of her aged cat,
Flounce.

On the occasion I am telling about, Mrs. Norton, who lives
alone in a vast old graystone apartment building known as
Hampton Court, was awakened three hours after midnight
by a knocking on her back door. Her back door leads out

into a treeless and rather dreary courtyard, as do all the other
back doors in the building. It is really four buildings joined
together and running around a whole block, with the courtyard in the center. Mrs. Norton looked out her bedroom
window and saw two women standing at her door below—
there was a faint light striking down from somewhere. She
was for a moment convinced that they were not live women,
but this conviction was dispelled when one of them called
up to her. Mrs. Norton then recognized the voice of a Mrs.
Stokes, a portly, jolly, gray-haired woman, also a resident of
Hampton Court, which is inhabited largely by old ladies

who are alone in the world. "Something terrible has happened," said Mrs. Stokes. The other woman did not say anything and did not look up. Mrs. Norton had the impression that she was weeping. She told them to wait a moment, pulled a wrapper around herself, and went down and let them in.

It came out that the father of the other woman, a Mrs. Phelps, who had just recently moved into Hampton Court, had dropped dead a few minutes before in her apartment. He had come to visit her that day and now he was dead. Mrs. Phelps, a mild little old woman with white hair, sobbed quietly. It seemed that she had run instantly to Mrs. Stokes, her nearest neighbor in the building, and Mrs. Stokes had suggested that they get Mrs. Norton before going to the old man, because Mrs. Norton was psychic and therefore just the person to turn to in the event of sudden death before dawn. Mrs. Phelps said that she had heard her father fall in his bedroom and, rushing in, had found that he was dead. She was sure that he was dead—there was no need to call a doctor; but would Mrs. Norton telephone for an—an undertaker?

Mrs. Norton, not yet fully awake, suggested that it might be a good idea to make the ladies some tea. Tea was a quieting thing and the brewing of it would give Mrs. Norton a while to think. Mrs. Phelps said that she would take pleasure in a cup of tea. So Mrs. Norton made the tea and the three ladies each drank a cup of it, slowly, talking of other things than the tragedy. Mrs. Phelps seemed to feel much better. Mrs. Norton then wanted to know if there was any particular undertaker that Mrs. Phelps would like to call in and Mrs. Phelps named one, whom I shall call Bellinger. So Mrs. Norton phoned Bellinger's, and a sleepy voice answered and said a man would be right over to Mrs. Phelps' apartment. At this Mrs. Phelps said, "I think I would like to go back to father alone for a moment. Would you ladies be kind enough to come over in a little while?" Mrs. Norton said they would be over as soon as she got dressed, and Mrs. Phelps left. "She seems very sweet," said Mrs. Stokes. "It's the first time I've really talked to her. It's very sad. And at this time of the night, too." Mrs. Norton said that it was a terrible thing, but that, of course, it was to be expected, since Mrs. Phelps' father must have been a very old man, for Mrs. Phelps looked to be sixty-five at least.

When Mrs. Norton was dressed, the two ladies went out into the bleak courtyard and made their way slowly across it and knocked at the back door of Mrs. Phelps' apartment. There was no answer. They knocked more loudly, taking turns, and then together, and there was still no answer. They could see a light inside, but they heard no sound. Bewildered and alarmed (for Mrs. Phelps had not seemed deaf), the two ladies went through Mrs. Stokes' apartment, which was right next door, and around to Mrs. Phelps' front door and rang the bell. It rang loudly and they rang it many times, but no one came to the door. There was a light on in the hall. They could not hear anyone moving inside.

It was at this juncture that Bellinger's man arrived, a small, grumpy man whose overcoat was too large for him. He took over the ringing of the bell and rang it many times, insistently, but without success. Then, grumbling to himself, he turned the doorknob and the door opened and the three walked into the hallway. Mrs. Norton called and then Mrs. Stokes called and then Bellinger's man shouted, but there was no other sound. The ladies looked at Bellinger's man in frank twittery fright. He said he would take a look around. They heard him going from room to room, opening and closing doors, first downstairs and then upstairs, now and then calling out "Madam!" He came back downstairs into the hallway where the ladies were and said there was nobody in the place, dead or alive. He was angry. After all, he had been roused out of his sleep. He said he believed the whole thing was a practical joke, and a damned bad practical joke, if you asked him. The ladies assured him it was not a joke, but he said "Bah" and walked to the door. There he turned and faced them with his hand on the knob and announced that in thirty-three years with Bellinger this was the first and only time he had ever been called out on a case in which there was no corpse, the first and only time. Then he strode out the door, jumped into his car, and drove off. The ladies hurried out of the apartment after him.

They went back to Mrs. Norton's apartment and made some more tea and talked in excited whispers about the curious happenings of the night. Mrs. Stokes said she did not know Mrs. Phelps very well but that she seemed to be a pleasant and kindly neighbor. Mrs. Norton said that she had known her only to nod to but that she had seemed very nice. Mrs. Stokes wondered whether they should call the police, but Mrs. Norton said that the police would be of no earthly use on what was obviously a psychic case. The ladies would go to bed and get some sleep and go over to Mrs. Phelps' apartment when it was daylight. Mrs. Stokes said she didn't feel like going back to her apartment—she would have to pass Mrs. Phelps' apartment on the way—so Mrs. Norton said she could sleep in her extra bed.

The two women, worn out by their experience, fell asleep shortly and did not wake up until almost ten o'clock. They hurriedly got up and dressed and went over to Mrs. Phelps' back door, on which Mrs. Norton knocked. The door opened and Mrs. Phelps stood there, smiling. She was fully dressed and did not look grief-stricken or tired. "Well!" she said. "This *is* nice! Do come in!" They went in. Mrs. Phelps led them into the living room, a neat and well-ordered room, and asked them to take chairs. They sat down, each on the edge of her chair, and waited. Mrs. Phelps talked pleasantly of this and that. Did they ever see anything grow like her giant begonia in the window? She had grown it from a slip that a Mrs. Bricker had given her. Had they heard that the Chalmers child was down with the measles? The other ladies murmured responses now and then and finally rose and said that they must be going. Mrs. Phelps asked them to run in any time; it had been so sweet of them to call. They went out into the courtyard and walked all the way to Mrs. Norton's door without a word, and there they stopped and stared at each other.

That, aggravatingly enough, is where Mrs. Norton's story ended—except for the bit of information that Mrs. Stokes, frightened of Mrs. Phelps, had moved away from Hampton Court a week after the night of alarm. Mrs. Norton does not believe in probing into the psychic. One must take, gratefully, such glimpses of the psychic as are presented to one, and seek no further. She had no theories as to what happened to Mrs. Phelps after Mrs. Phelps "went back to her father." The disappearance fitted snugly into the whole pattern of the night and she let it go at that. Mrs. Norton and Mrs. Phelps have become quite good friends now, and Mrs. Phelps frequently drops in for tea. They have had no further adventures. Mrs. Phelps has not mentioned her father since that night. All that Mrs. Norton really knows about her is that she was born in Bellefontaine, Ohio, and sometimes wishes that she were back there. I took the story for what it was, fuzzy edges and all: an almost perfect example of what goes on in the life that moves slowly about the lonely figure of Mrs. Jessie Norton, reading the precarious future in her tea leaves, listening to the whisperings and knockings of the ominous present at her door. Before I left her she read my fortune in the teacup I had drunk from. It seems that a slight, blonde woman is going to come into my life and that I should beware of the sea.

17. Guns and Game Calls

I WANDERED INTO STOEGER'S FAMOUS GUN HOUSE IN FIFTH
Avenue the other morning to see if they could repair my
derringer. The way I came to have a derringer is rather odd
and quite unlike me, really. I had been up in Winsted,
Connecticut, and on the way back I stopped my car in front
of a little shop in the town. In the window, on a table, lay
the derringer. It was a very old derringer. As you may know,
a derringer is a small knob-handled, short-barreled pistol with
which ladies and gentlemen used to shoot at one another in
the old days. The one I came upon had been found, the man
in the shop told me, on Canaan Mountain by a Sunday
wanderer a few weeks before. It had lain there in the rains
and snows of many years, dropped perhaps by a tired soldier
or a fallen duellist. It bore the number 247 in the iron of its
barrel, showing that it was one of the very earliest derringers.
The man said it was in firing condition and, sure enough,
it cocked with a smart click and the hammer fell with a
smart click when I pulled the trigger. I bought it for five
dollars and brought it to New York, where for more than
a week I carried it about with me wherever I went, clicking
it at people. Finally I wore the trigger spring out and it
wouldn't work any more, so when I was passing Stoeger's
the other day, I thought I would go in and ask whether
they could repair it.

I know very little about guns, the old derringer being the
first gun I have ever owned. Therefore I was a bit awed

and uneasy to find myself standing at a counter in Stoeger's facing a muscular, keen-eyed salesman who, I discerned at a glance, knew all about guns. In a hasty look around, as he asked me crisply what he could do for me, I noticed that there did not appear to be, in the whole store, any old guns such as you find on mountains. Everything was modern, shiningly new, elaborately chased and engraved, and apparently expensive (I found out later that a new Luger costs

European Oystercatcher

$100, in case you were thinking of giving anyone a new Luger). Well, there I was, facing this muscular, keen-eyed salesman who knew all about guns, from King micrometered autolocking peep-sights (price $4.50) to the Paragon 236E de luxe special over-and-under shotgun (price $1,150). (I'll tell later how I happen to know the names and prices of those things.)

"It's—ah—it's about a derringer," I said finally, in a low and confidential tone. The man led me promptly, without a word, to a long glass showcase and brought out of it a derringer, a brand-new Remington double-barrelled, two-shot, rim-fire derringer. I looked it over frowningly, felt its weight, sighted along the barrel, and put it back on the counter. I was in a considerable predicament because I didn't want to buy a new derringer and I had led the salesman to believe that I did. I was too timid, of course, to bring up now the subject of my old, rusty, single-barrelled, one-shot, powder-and-ball, flint-fired, mountain-found derringer. The moment for that had gone by. I finally got out of the predicament when he brought up the question of a pistol permit. I haven't got one, of course, and that let me out. I was about to creep away when I noticed a pile of Stoeger's "Catalog and Handbook" on the counter. They cost fifty cents each and I bought one—it seemed the least that I could do.

American Derringer

Every man, I think now, should own a gun catalog and handbook. I spent the whole evening going through mine, from Enfield rifles to Webley automatics, and I know enough names and facts and figures and calibres to impress, if not the average member of what Stoeger's calls "the shooting fraternity," at least the average Desdemona one is likely to encounter in the metropolitan area. I know just off-hand, for instance, that you can buy a Harrington & Richardson vest-pocket revolver that weighs only eight ounces and has a barrel only 1⅛ inches long, just the thing for a lady to slip into her evening bag when she goes up to see her escort's etchings after the opera. I know a lot of other things, too, but I am saving them all for dinner-table small talk. All, that is, except what I know about English and American game calls. That knowledge I am willing to share with people because it is too complicated for dinner-table small talk and because I am generous enough to let people in on what may solve some of their Christmas-list problems. Not everybody is going to give a set of English and American game calls this season, and whoever does is likely to be thought of among his friends as a sophisticated and ingenious fellow.

Stoeger's then, has stocked sets of fifteen different game calls, twelve English and three American. They are of various shapes and sizes, and look like everything from a patrolman's whistle to something that has been accidentally wrenched off a camshaft (the pheasant and screech-owl call, for example). If you own the whole set of fifteen game calls, you can call all the following creatures: pheasant, screech owl, quail, blackbird, stoat, stag, heath hen (don't waste your breath on this one), moor hen, water hen, grouse, rabbit, fox, partridge, lapwing, hawk, buzzard owl, duck, teal, widgeon, snipe, redshank, sandpiper, goose, turkey, lark, woodcock, and oystercatcher.

Not everyone, of course, is going to be able to call all of these birds and beasts offhand, the way he might shoot dice. To manipulate a game call expertly requires, I could see by the catalog, not only skill and practice but, I suspect, a natural inborn gift, or frenzy. Take the English snipe call, for example. This is an instrument that looks like a combination biscuit-cutter and fountain pen, and it is, I gather, as difficult to play upon as a saxophone. On it you can call not only the snipe but the redshank, sandpiper, and oystercatcher (an oystercatcher is a water bird that catches oysters). Says the catalog: "Redshank: render a series of plaintive, whistling notes by placing the tongue against mouthpiece of whistle and giving five short, sharp blasts, terminating suddenly. Sandpiper: note is similar to redshank only longer and more trilling, interspersed by low, mournful notes." None of us, I think, is going to become proficient enough on the snipe call to get a redshank and then a sandpiper in quick succession, and I, for one, am not even going to try to summon an oystercatcher, much as I would like to see one, because to do that, the catalog says, you must give "a strong, sharp note, made by removing the tongue and quickly replacing it," a little feat that died with Houdini.

On the stag call, which looks like a darning egg, one must produce "a long blow, increasing and then dying down (similar to a cow's 'low')." Stay away, I should advise, from that one. It is extremely difficult to get within earshot of a stag, and the stag-caller is bound to be in constant danger of finding himself entirely surrounded by cows, or, what is worse, bulls. The English rabbit call (the only American calls are the turkey, duck, and American snipe) leaves me somewhat confused because it apparently does not attract rabbits at all, but foxes. "With a little practice," says the catalog, "a lifelike imitation of a rabbit can be obtained which acts as an excellent fox decoy." The sound made is a high-pitched squeal, which is not, I suppose, the way one rabbit attracts another rabbit. Most of the foxhunters I know are lusty, florid fellows who hunt foxes in the great tradition of "View hallo!" and "There goes the —— now!" I can't somehow picture any foxhunter I have ever seen standing in a woodsy dell and squealing like a rabbit. And this call, mind you, is an English call! Maybe they are softening up over there.

Passing over the stoat and the widgeon, which I am pleased to regard merely as a bit of mild Stoeger spoofing, I pause, in concluding my survey, to warn you against the lark call. I happen to know the case history of one man who used a lark call. He was a Frenchman who lived near Nice, and the brief and unhappy account of his lark hunt got into the candid pages of the invaluable *Éclaireur de Nice et du Sud-Est* some ten years ago when I was sojourning on the Riviera. It seems that this gentleman climbed a tree and, having cunningly concealed himself in the foliage, began blowing on his lark call—"short, sharp in and out breaths, varying with buzzing sound in mouth at same time," says the catalog (try that on your lark call). Well, this man was so good that he was suddenly riddled with shotgun slugs from the weapon of another hunter, who had been royally taken in by the remarkable imitation. The thing to do with your English and American game-call set is simply to put it away somewhere in your den and think of it as an interesting collection, like so many old derringers. Nobody wants to get shot for a lark, or gored by an unsympathetic and disillusioned bull.

18. The Hiding Generation

ONE AFTERNOON ALMOST TWO YEARS AGO, AT A COCKTAIL PARTY (at least, this is the way I have been telling the story), an eager middle-aged woman said to me, "Do you belong to the Lost Generation, Mr. T?" and I retorted, coldly and quick as a flash, "No, Madam, I belong to the Hiding Generation."

As a matter of fact, no woman ever asked me such a question at a cocktail party or anywhere else. I thought up the little dialogue one night when I couldn't sleep. At the time, my retort seemed pretty sharp and satirical to me, and I hoped that some day somebody *would* ask me if I belonged to the Lost Generation, so that I could say no, I belonged to the Hiding Generation. But nobody ever has. My retort, however, began working in the back of my mind. I decided that since I was apparently never going to get a chance to use it as repartee, I ought to do something else with it, if only to get it out of the back of my mind. About ten months ago I got around to the idea of writing a book called "The Hiding Generation," which would be the story of my own intellectual conflicts, emotional disturbances, spiritual adventures, and journalistic experiences, something in the manner of Malcolm Cowley's "Exile's Return" or Vincent Sheean's "Personal History." The notion seemed to me a remarkably good one, and I was quite excited by it. I bought a new typewriter ribbon and a ream of fresh copy paper; I sharpened a dozen pencils; I got a pipe and tobacco. Then I sat down at the typewriter, lighted my pipe, and wrote on a sheet of paper "The

178

Hiding Generation, by James Thurber." That was as far as I got, because I discovered that I could not think of anything else to say. I mean anything at all.

Thus passed the first five or six hours of my work on the book. In the late afternoon some people dropped in for cocktails, and I didn't get around to the book again for two more

Some People Dropped in for Cocktails

days. Then I found that I still didn't have anything to say. I wondered if I had already said everything I had to say, but I decided, in looking over what I had said in the past, that I really hadn't ever said anything. This was an extremely depressing thought, and for a while I considered going into some other line of work. But I am not fitted for any other line of work, by inclination, experience, or aptitude. There was consequently nothing left for me but to go back to work on "The Hiding Generation." I decided to "write it in my mind," in the manner of Arnold Bennett (who did practically all of "The Old Wives' Tale" in his head), and this I devoted myself to for about seven months. At length I sat down at the type-writer once more, and there I was again, tapping my fingers on the table, lighting and relighting my pipe, getting up every now and then for a drink of water. I figured finally that maybe I had better make an outline of the book; probably all the writers I had in mind—and there was a pretty big list of them now, including Walter Duranty and Negley Farson—had made an outline of what they were going to say, using Roman numerals for the main divisions and small letters "a" and "b," etc., for the subdivisions. So I set down some Roman numerals and small letters on a sheet of paper. First I wrote "I. Early Youth." I could think of no subdivisions to go under that, so I put down "II. Young Manhood." All I could think of to go under that was "a. Studs Lonigan." Obviously that wouldn't do, so I tore up the sheet of paper and put the whole thing by for another week.

During that week I was tortured by the realization that I couldn't think of anything important that had happened to me up to the time I was thirty-three and began raising Scotch terriers. The conviction that nothing important had happened to me until I was thirty-three, that I had apparently had no intellectual conflicts or emotional disturbances, or anything, reduced me to such a state of dejection that I decided to go to Bridgeport for a few days and stay all alone in a hotel room. The motivation behind this decision is still a little vague in my mind, but I think it grew out of a feeling that I wasn't worthy of going away to Florida or Bermuda or Nassau or any other nice place. I had Bridgeport "coming to me," in a sense, as retribution for my blank youth and my blank young manhood. In the end, of course, I did not go to Bridgeport. I took a new sheet of paper and began another outline.

This time I started out with "I. University Life. a. Intel-lectual Conflicts." No other workable subdivisions occurred to me. The only Emotional Disturbance that came to my mind was unworthy of being incorporated in the book, for it had to do with the moment, during the Phi Psi May Dance of 1917, when I knocked a fruit salad onto the floor. The incident was as bald as that, and somehow I couldn't correlate it with anything. To start out with such an episode and then just leave it hanging in the air would not give the reader anything to get his teeth into. Therefore I concentrated on "Intellectual Conflicts," but I could not seem to call up any which had torn my mind asunder during my college days. Yet there *must* have been some. I made a lot of little squares and circles with a pencil for half an hour, and finally I remembered one intellectual conflict—if you could call it that. It was really only an argument I had had with a classmate at Ohio State University named Arthur Spencer, about "Tess of the D'Urbervilles." I had taken the view that the hero of the book was not justified in running away to South America and abandoning Tess simply because she had been indiscreet in her youth. Spencer, on the other hand, contended the man was fully justified, and that he (Spencer) would have run away to South America and left Tess, or any other woman, under the circumstances—that is, if he had had the money. As a matter of fact, Spencer settled down in East Liverpool, Ohio, where he is partner in his father's hardware store, and married a very nice girl named Sarah Gammadinger, who had been a Kappa at Ohio State.

I came to the conclusion finally that I would have to leave my university life out of the book, along with my early youth and young manhood. Therefore, my next Roman numeral, which would normally have been IV, automatically became I. I placed after it the words "Paris: A New World. a. Thoughts at Sea." It happened that upon leaving the university, in 1918, I went to Paris as a clerk, Grade B, in the Ameri-

can Embassy. In those days I didn't call it clerk, Grade B, I
called it attaché, but it seemed to me that the honest and
forceful thing to do was to tell the truth. The book would
have more power and persuasion if I told the truth—providing I could remember the truth. There was a lot I couldn't
remember, I found out in trying to. For instance, I had put
down "Thoughts at Sea" after "a" because I couldn't recall
anything significant that had happened to me during the five
months I spent in Washington, D. C., before sailing for
France. (Furthermore, it didn't seem logical to put a sub-
division called "Washington Days" under a general heading
called "Paris: A New World.") Something, of course, must
have happened to me in Washington, something provocative
or instructive, something that added to my stature, but all
that comes back to me is a series of paltry little memories. I
remember there was a waitress in the Post Café, at the corner
of Thirteenth and E Streets, whose last name was Rabbit.
I've forgot her first name and even what she looked like,
but her last name was Rabbit. A Mrs. Rabbit. Then there was
the flu epidemic, during which I gargled glycothymoline
three times a day. All the rest has gone from me.

I found I could remember quite a lot about my days at
sea on my way to Paris: A New World. In the first place, I
had bought a box of San Felice cigars to take with me on the
transport, but I was seasick all the way over and the cigars
were smoked by a man named Ed Corcoran, who travelled
with me. He was not sick a day. I believe he said he had
never been sick a day in his life. Even some of the sailors
were sick, but not Corcoran. No, sir. He was constantly in and
out of our stateroom, singing, joking, smoking my cigars.
The other thing I remembered about the voyage was that
my trunk and suitcase failed to get on the ship; they were put
by mistake on some other ship—the Minnetonka, perhaps, or

the Charles O. Sprague, a coastwise fruit steamer. In any case, I didn't recover them until May, 1920, in Paris, and the Hershey bars my mother had packed here and there in both the trunk and the suitcase had melted and were all over everything. All my suits were brown, even the gray one. But I am anticipating myself. All this belongs under "Paris: A New World. b. Paris."

I was just twenty-five when I first saw Paris, and I was still a little sick. Unfortunately, when I try to remember my first impressions of Paris and the things that happened to me, I get them mixed up with my second trip to Paris, which was seven years later, when I was feeling much better and really got around more. On that first trip to Paris I was, naturally enough, without any clothes, except what I had on, and I had to outfit myself at once, which I did at the Galeries Lafayette. I paid $4.75 in American money for a pair of B.V.D.s. I remember that, all right. Nothing else comes back to me very clearly; everything comes back to me all jumbled up. I tried about five times to write down a comprehensive outline of my experiences in Paris: A New World, but the thing remained sketchy and trivial. If there was any development in my character or change in my outlook on life during that phase, I forget just where it came in and why. So I cut out the Paris interlude.

I find, in looking over my accumulation of outlines, that my last attempt to get the volume started began with the heading "I. New York Again: An Old World." This was confusing, because it could have meaning and pertinence only if it followed the chapter outlined as "Paris: A New World," and that had all been eliminated along with my Early Youth, Young Manhood, and University Days. Moreover, while my life back in New York must have done a great deal to change my character, viewpoint, objectives, and political ideals, I forget just exactly how this happened. I am the kind of man who should keep notes about such things. If I do not keep notes, I simply cannot remember a thing. Oh, I remember odds and ends, as you have seen, but they certainly would not tie up into anything like a moving chronicle of a man's life, running to a hundred and fifty thousand words. If they ran to twenty-five hundred words, I would be going good. Now, it's a funny thing: catch me in a drawing-room, over the coffee and liqueurs, particularly the Scotch-and-sodas, and I could hold you, or at least keep talking to you, for five or six hours about my life, but somebody would have to take down what I said and organize it into a book. When I sit down to *write* the story of my life, all I can think of is Mrs. Rabbit, and the Hershey bars, and the B.V.D.'s that came within two bits of costing five bucks. That is, of course, until I get up to the time when I was thirty-three and began raising Scotch terriers. I can put down all of that, completely and movingly, without even making an outline. Naturally, as complete and as moving as it might be, it would scarcely make a biography like, say, Negley Farson's, and it certainly would not sustain so pretentious a title as "The Hiding Generation." I would have to publish it as a pamphlet entitled "The Care and Training of Scotch Terriers." I am very much afraid that that is what my long arduous struggle to write the story of my life is going to come down to, if it is going to come down to anything.

Well, all of us cannot write long autobiographies. But *almost* all of us can.

19. *Wild Bird Hickok and His Friends*

IN ONE OF THE MANY INTERESTING ESSAYS THAT MAKE UP HIS book called "Abinger Harvest," Mr. E. M. Forster, discussing what he sees when he is reluctantly dragged to the movies in London, has set down a sentence that fascinates me. It is: "American women shoot the hippopotamus with eyebrows made of platinum." I have given that remarkable sentence a great deal of study, but I still do not know whether Mr. Forster means that American women have platinum eyebrows or that the hippopotamus has platinum eyebrows or that American women shoot platinum eyebrows into the hippopotamus. At any rate, it faintly stirred in my mind a dim train of elusive memories which were brightened up suddenly and brought into sharp focus for me when, one night, I went to see "The Plainsman," a hard-riding, fast-shooting movie dealing with warfare in the Far West back in the bloody seventies. I knew then what Mr. Forster's curious and tantalizing sentence reminded me of. It was like nothing in the world so much as certain sentences which appeared in a group of French paperback dime (or, rather, twenty-five-centime) novels that I collected a dozen years ago in France. "The Plainsman" brought up these old pulp thrillers in all clarity for me because, like that movie, they dealt mainly with the stupendous activities of Buffalo Bill and Wild Bill Hickok;

but in them were a unique fantasy, a special inventiveness, and an imaginative abandon beside which the movie treatment of the two heroes pales, as the saying goes, into nothing. In moving from one apartment to another some years ago, I somehow lost my priceless collection of *contes héroïques du Far-Ouest*, but happily I find that a great many of the deathless adventures of the French Buffalo Bill and Wild Bill Hickok remain in my memory. I hope that I shall recall them, for anodyne, when with eyes too dim to read, I pluck finally at the counterpane.

In the first place, it should perhaps be said that in the eighteen-nineties the American dime-novel hero who appears to have been most popular with the French youth—and adult —given to such literature was Nick Carter. You will find somewhere in one of John L. Stoddard's published lectures— there used to be a set in almost every Ohio bookcase—an anecdote about how an American tourist, set upon by *apaches* in a dark *rue* in Paris in the nineties, caused them to scatter in terror merely by shouting, *"Je suis Nick Carter!"* But at the turn of the century, or shortly thereafter, Buffalo Bill became the favorite. Whether he still is or not, I don't know—perhaps Al Capone or John Dillinger has taken his place. Twelve years ago, however, he was going great guns—or perhaps I should say great dynamite, for one of the things I most clearly remember about the Buffalo Bill of the French authors was that he always carried with him sticks of dynamite which, when he was in a particularly tough spot—that is, surrounded by more than two thousand Indians—he hurled into their midst, destroying them by the hundred. Many of the most inspired paperbacks that I picked up in my quest were used ones I found in those little stalls along the Seine. It was there, for instance, that I came across one of my favorites, "Les Aventures du Wild Bill dans le Far-Ouest."

Wild Bill Hickok was, in this wonderful and beautiful tale, an even more prodigious manipulator of the six-gun than he seems to have been in real life, which, as you must know, is saying a great deal. He frequently mowed down a hundred or two hundred Indians in a few minutes with his redoubtable pistol. The French author of this masterpiece for some mysterious but delightful reason referred to Hickok

"Vous vous Promenez Très Tard ce Soir, Mon Vieux!"

sometimes as Wild Bill and sometimes as Wild Bird. *"Bonjour, Wild Bill!"* his friend Buffalo Bill often said to him when they met, only to shout a moment later, *"Regardez, Wild Bird! Les Peaux-Rouges!"* The two heroes spent a great deal of their time, as in "The Plainsman," helping each other out of dreadful situations. Once, for example, while hunting Seminoles in Florida, Buffalo Bill fell into a tiger trap that had been set for him by the Indians—he stepped onto what turned out to be sticks covered with grass, and plunged to the bottom of a deep pit. At this point our author wrote, *" 'Mercy me!' s'écria Buffalo Bill."* The great scout was rescued, of course, by none other than Wild Bill, or Bird, who, emerging from the forest to see his old comrade in distress, could only exclaim *"My word!"*

It was, I believe, in another volume that one of the most interesting characters in all French fiction of the Far West appeared, a certain Major Preston, alias Preeton, alias Preslon (the paperbacks rarely spelled anyone's name twice in succession the same way). This hero, we were told when he was introduced, "had distinguished himself in the Civil War by capturing Pittsburgh," a feat which makes Lee's invasion of Pennsylvania seem mere child's play. Major Preeton (I always preferred that alias) had come out West to fight the Indians with cannon, since he believed it absurd that nobody had thought to blow them off the face of the earth with cannon before. How he made out with his artillery against the forest skulkers I have forgotten, but I have an indelible memory of a certain close escape that Buffalo Bill had in this same book. It seems that, through an oversight, he had set out on a scouting trip without his dynamite—he also carried, by the way, cheroots and a flashlight—and hence, when he stumbled upon a huge band of redskins, he had to ride as fast as he could for the nearest fort. He made it just in time. "Buffalo Bill," ran the story, "clattered across the drawbridge and into the fort just ahead of the Indians, who, unable to stop in time, plunged into the moat and were drowned." It may have been in this same tale that Buffalo Bill was once so hard pressed that he had to send for Wild Bird to help him out. Usually, when one was in trouble, the other showed up by a kind of instinct, but this time Wild Bird was nowhere to be found. It was a long time, in fact, before his whereabouts were discovered. You will never guess where he was. He was "taking the baths at Atlantic City under orders of his physician." But he came riding across the country in one day to Buffalo Bill's side, and all was well. Major Preeton, it sticks in my mind, got bored with the service in the Western hotels and went "back to Philadelphia" (Philadelphia appears to have been the capital city of the United States at this time). The Indians in all these tales—and this is probably what gave Major Preeton his great idea—were seldom seen as individuals or in pairs or small groups, but prowled about in well-ordered columns of squads. I recall, however, one drawing (the paperbacks were copiously illustrated) which showed two *Peaux-Rouges* leaping upon and capturing a scout who had wandered too far from his drawbridge one night. The picture represented one of the Indians as smilingly taunting his captive, and the caption read, *"Vous vous promenez très tard ce soir, mon vieux!"* This remained my favorite line until I saw one night in Paris an old W. S. Hart movie called "Le Roi du Far-Ouest," in which Hart, insulted by a drunken ruffian, turned upon him and said, in his grim, laconic way, *"Et puis, après?"*

I first became interested in the French tales of the Far West when, one winter in Nice, a French youngster of fifteen, who, it turned out, devoted all his spending money to them, asked me if I had ever seen a "wishtonwish." This meant nothing to me, and I asked him where he had heard about the wishtonwish. He showed me a Far West paperback he was reading. There was a passage in it which recounted an adventure of Buffalo Bill and Wild Bill during the course of which Buffalo Bill signalled to Wild Bird "in the voice of the wishtonwish." Said the author in a parenthesis which at that time gave me as much trouble as Mr. Forster's sentence about the platinum eyebrows does now, "The wishtonwish was seldom heard west of Philadelphia." It was some time—indeed, it was not until I got back to America—that I traced the wishtonwish to its lair, and in so doing discovered the influence of James Fenimore Cooper on all these French writers of Far

West tales. Cooper, in his novels, frequently mentioned the wishtonwish, which was a Caddoan Indian name for the prairie dog. Cooper erroneously applied it to the whippoorwill. An animal called the "ouapiti" also figured occasionally in the French stories, and this turned out to be the wapiti, or American elk, also mentioned in Cooper's tales. The French writer's parenthetical note on the habitat of the wishtonwish only added to the delightful confusion and inaccuracy which threaded these wondrous stories.

There were, in my lost and lamented collection, a hundred other fine things, which I have forgotten, but there is one that will forever remain with me. It occurred in a book in which, as I remember it, Billy the Kid, alias Billy the Boy, was the central figure. At any rate, two strangers had turned up in a small Western town and their actions had aroused the suspicions of a group of respectable citizens, who forthwith called on the sheriff to complain about the newcomers. The sheriff listened gravely for a while, got up and buckled on his gun belt, and said, *"Alors, je vais demander ses cartes d'identité!"* There are few things, in any literature, that have ever given me a greater thrill than coming across that line.

20. *Doc Marlowe*

I WAS TOO YOUNG TO BE OTHER THAN AWED AND PUZZLED BY Doc Marlowe when I knew him. I was only sixteen when he died. He was sixty-seven. There was that vast difference in our ages and there was a vaster difference in our backgrounds. Doc Marlowe was a medicine-show man. He had been a lot of other things, too: a circus man, the proprietor of a concession at Coney Island, a saloon-keeper; but in his fifties he had traveled around with a tent-show troupe made up of a Mexican named Chickalilli, who threw knives, and a man called Professor Jones, who played the banjo. Doc Marlowe would come out after the entertainment and harangue the crowd and sell bottles of medicine for all kinds of ailments. I found out all this about him gradually, toward the last, and after he died. When I first knew him, he represented the Wild West to me, and there was nobody I admired so much.

I met Doc Marlowe at old Mrs. Willoughby's rooming house. She had been a nurse in our family, and I used to go and visit her over week-ends sometimes, for I was very fond of her. I was about eleven years old then. Doc Marlowe wore scarred leather leggings, a bright-colored bead vest that he said he got from the Indians, and a ten-gallon hat with kitchen matches stuck in the band, all the way around. He was about six feet four inches tall, with big shoulders, and a long, drooping mustache. He let his hair grow long, like General Custer's. He had a wonderful collection of Indian relics and six-shooters, and he used to tell me stories of his

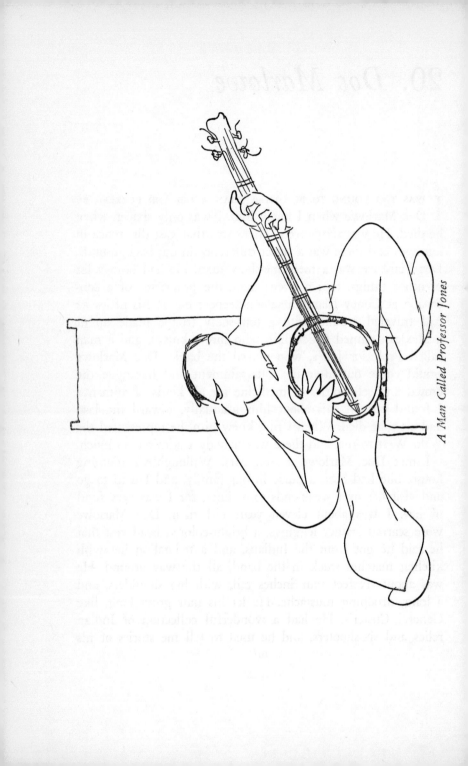

A Man Called Professor Jones

adventures in the Far West. His favorite expressions were "Hay, boy!" and "Hay, boy-gie!," which he used the way some people now use "Hot dog!" or "Doggone!" He told me once that he had killed an Indian chief named Yellow Hand in a tomahawk duel on horseback. I thought he was the great-est man I had ever seen. It wasn't until he died and his son came on from New Jersey for the funeral that I found out he had never been in the Far West in his life. He had been born in Brooklyn.

Doc Marlowe had given up the road when I knew him, but he still dealt in what he called "medicines." His stock in trade was a liniment that he had called Snake Oil when he travelled around. He changed the name to Blackhawk Lini-ment when he settled in Columbus. Doc didn't always sell enough of it to pay for his bed and board, and old Mrs. Willoughby would sometimes have to "trust" him for weeks at a time. She didn't mind, because his liniment had taken a bad kink out of her right limb that had bothered her for thirty years. I used to see people whom Doc had massaged with Blackhawk Liniment move arms and legs that they hadn't been able to move before he "treated" them. His patients were day laborers, wives of streetcar conductors, and people like that. Sometimes they would shout and weep after Doc had massaged them, and several got up and walked around who hadn't been able to walk before. One man hadn't turned his head to either side for seven years before Doc soused him with Blackhawk. In half an hour he could move his head as easily as I could move mine. "Glory be to God!" he shouted. "It's the secret qualities in the ointment, my friend," Doc Marlowe told him, suavely. He always called the liniment ointment.

News of his miracles got around by word of mouth among the poorer classes of town—he was not able to reach the better people (the "tony folks," he called them)— but there was never a big enough sale to give Doc a steady income. For one thing, people thought there was more magic in Doc's touch than in his liniment, and, for another, the ingredients of Blackhawk cost so much that his profits were not very great. I know, because I used to go to the wholesale chemical company once in a while for him and buy his supplies. Everything that went into the liniment was standard and expensive (and well-known, not secret). A man at the company told me he didn't see how Doc could make much money on it at thirty-five cents a bottle. But even when he was very low in funds Doc never cut out any of the ingredients or substituted cheaper ones. Mrs. Willoughby had suggested it to him once, she told me, when she was helping him "put up a batch," and he had got mad. "He puts a heap of store by that liniment being right up to the mark," she said.

Doc added to his small earnings, I discovered, by money he made gambling. He used to win quite a few dollars on Saturday nights at Freck's saloon, playing poker with the market-men and the railroaders who dropped in there. It wasn't for several years that I found out Doc cheated. I had never heard about marked cards until he told me about them and showed me his. It was one rainy afternoon, after he had played seven-up with Mrs. Willoughby and old Mr. Peiffer, another roomer of hers. They had played for small stakes (Doc wouldn't play cards unless there was some money up, and Mrs. Willoughby wouldn't play if very much was up). Only twenty or thirty cents had changed hands in the end. Doc had won it all. I remember my astonishment and indignation when it dawned on me that Doc had used the marked cards in playing the old lady and the old man. "You didn't cheat *them*, did you?" I asked him. "Jimmy, my boy," he told me, "the man that calls the turn wins the money." His eyes twinkled and he seemed to enjoy my anger. I was outraged, but I was helpless. I knew I could never tell Mrs. Willoughby about how Doc had cheated her at seven-up. I liked her, but I liked him, too. Once he had given me a whole dollar to buy fireworks with on the Fourth of July.

I remember once, when I was staying at Mrs. Willoughby's, Doc Marlowe was roused out of bed in the middle of the night by a poor woman who was frantic because her little girl was sick. This woman had had the sciatica driven out of her by his liniment, she reminded Doc. He placed her then. She had never been able to pay him a cent for his liniment or his "treatments," and he had given her a great many. He got up and dressed, and went over to her house. The child had colic, I suppose. Doc couldn't have had any idea what was the matter, but he sopped on liniment; he sopped on a whole bottle. When he came back home, two hours later, he said he had "relieved the distress." The little girl had gone to sleep and was all right the next day, whether on account of Doc Marlowe or in spite of him I don't know. "I want to thank you, Doctor," said the mother, tremulously, when she called on him that afternoon. He gave her another bottle of liniment, and he didn't charge her for it or for his "professional call." He used to massage, and give liniment to, a lot of sufferers who were too poor to pay. Mrs. Willoughby told him once that he was too generous and too easily taken in. Doc laughed —and winked at me, with the twinkle in his eye that he had had when he told me how he had cheated the old lady at cards.

Once I went for a walk with him out Town Street on a Saturday afternoon. It was a warm day, and after a while I said I wanted a soda. Well, he said, he didn't care if he took something himself. We went into a drugstore, and I ordered a chocolate soda and he had a lemon phosphate. When we had finished, he said, "Jimmy, my son, I'll match you to see who pays for the drinks." He handed me a quarter and he told me to toss the quarter and he would call the turn. He called heads and won. I paid for the drinks. It left me with a dime.

I was fifteen when Doc got out his pamphlets, as he called them. He had eased the misery of the wife of a small-time printer and the grateful man had given him a special price on two thousand advertising pamphlets. There was very little in them about Blackhawk Liniment. They were mostly about Doc himself and his "Life in the Far West." He had gone out to Franklin Park one day with a photographer—another of his numerous friends—and there the photographer took dozens of pictures of Doc, a lariat in one hand, a six-shooter in the other. I had gone along. When the pamphlets came out, there were the pictures of Doc, peering around trees, crouching behind bushes, whirling the lariat, aiming the gun. "Dr. H. M. Marlowe Hunting Indians" was one of the captions. "Dr. H. M. Marlowe after Hoss-Thieves" was another one. He was very proud of the pamphlets and always had a sheaf with him. He would pass them out to people on the street.

Two years before he died Doc got hold of an ancient, wheezy Cadillac somewhere. He aimed to start traveling around again, he said, but he never did, because the old automobile was so worn out it wouldn't hold up for more than a mile or so. It was about this time that a man named Hardman and his wife came to stay at Mrs. Willoughby's. They were farm people from around Lancaster who had sold their place. They got to like Doc because he was so jolly, they said, and they enjoyed his stories. He treated Mrs. Hardman for an old complaint in the small of her back and wouldn't take any money for it. They thought he was a fine gentleman. Then there came a day when they announced that they were going to St. Louis, where they had a son. They talked some of settling in St. Louis. Doc Marlowe told them they ought to buy a nice auto cheap and drive out, instead of going by train—it wouldn't cost much and they could see the country, give themselves a treat. Now, he knew where they could pick up just such a car.

Of course, he finally sold them the decrepit Cadillac—it had been stored away somewhere in the back of a garage whose owner kept it there for nothing because Doc had relieved his mother of a distress in the groins, as Doc explained it. I don't know just how the garage man doctored up the car, but he did. It actually chugged along pretty steadily when Doc took the Hardmans out for a trial spin. He told them he hated to part with it, but he finally let them have it for a hundred dollars. I knew, of course, and so did Doc, that it couldn't last many miles.

Doc got a letter from the Hardmans in St. Louis ten days later. They had had to abandon the old junk pile in West Jefferson, some fifteen miles out of Columbus. Doc read the letter aloud to me, peering over his glasses, his eyes twinkling, every now and then punctuating the lines with "Hay, boy!" and "Hay, boy-gie!" "I just want you to know, Dr. Marlowe," he read, "what I think of low-life swindlers like you [Hay, boy!] and that it will be a long day before I put my trust in a two-faced lyer and imposture again [Hay, boy-gie!]. The garrage man in W. Jefferson told us your old rattle-trap had been doctored up just to fool us. It was a low down dirty trick as no swine would play on a white man [Hay, boy!]." Far from being disturbed by the letter, Doc Marlowe was plainly amused. He took off his glasses, after he finished it and laughed, his hand to his brow and his eyes closed. I was pretty mad, because I had liked the Hardmans, and because they had liked him. Doc Marlowe put the letter carefully back into its envelope and tucked it away in his inside coat pocket, as if it were something precious. Then he picked up a pack of cards and began to lay out a solitaire hand. "Want to set in a little seven-up game, Jimmy?" he asked me. I was furious "Not with a cheater like you!" I shouted, and stamped out of the room, slamming the door. I could hear him chuckling to himself behind me.

The last time I saw Doc Marlowe was just a few days before he died. I didn't know anything about death, but I knew that he was dying when I saw him. His voice was very faint and his face was drawn; they told me he had a lot of pain. When I got ready to leave the room, he asked me to bring him a tin box that was on his bureau. I got it and handed it to him. He poked around in it for a while with unsteady fingers and finally found what he wanted. He handed it to me. It was a quarter, or rather it looked like a quarter, but it had heads on both sides. "Never let the other fella call the turn, Jimmy, my boy," said Doc, with a shadow of his old twinkle and the echo of his old chuckle. I still have the two-headed quarter. For a long time I didn't like to think about it, or about Doc Marlowe, but I do now.

21. *Food Fun for the Menfolk*

FIVE OR SIX WEEKS AGO, SOMEONE WHO SIGNED HIMSELF SIMPLY A Friend sent me a page torn from the Sunday magazine section of the *Herald Tribune*. "I thought this might interest you," he wrote. Unfortunately, he failed to mark the particular item he had in mind. On one side of the page was an article called "New Thoughts about Awnings," which, naturally, didn't interest me at all. I turned the page over and came to this announcement: "Why shouldn't you be among the prize winners in our reader-recipe contest for dishes made with plain or prepared gelatin?" The answer to that was so simple as to be silly, so I went on to another column and a recipe for "Plum Surprise." That couldn't have been what A Friend wanted me to see, for the least of my interests in this world, the least of anybody's interests, is Plum Surprise. Gradually, by this process of elimination, I came to an article called "Shower Parties, Up-to-Date!" (the exclamation point is the author's). This was without doubt what A Friend wished to bring to my attention. I read the article with mingled feelings of dismay and downright dread and then threw it away. But it haunted me for weeks. I realized finally that "Shower Parties, Up-to-Date!" presented one of those menaces which it is far better to face squarely than to try to ignore, so I dug it up again and you and I are now going to face it together.

If we all stand as one, we can put a stop to the ominous innovation in shower parties which the author of the article, Miss Elizabeth Harriman, so gaily suggests.

It is Miss Elizabeth Harriman's contention that *it is high time to invite the bridegroom and his men friends to shower parties for the bride!* (The italics and the exclamation point are mine.) "Nowadays," she says, flatly, "the groom insists

The Hostess Hands Each Guest, Including Joe, a Piece of Cardboard

on being included in the party." Without descending to invective, mud-slinging, or the lie direct, I can only say that you and I and Miss Harriman have never met a groom and, what is more, are never going to meet a groom who insists on being included in a shower party given for his bride. A groom would as soon wear a veil and carry a bouquet of lilies of the valley and baby's-breath as attended a shower party. Particularly the kind of shower party which Miss Harriman, with fiendish glee, goes on to invent right out of her own head. Let her start it off for you herself: "After supper—which should be simple—comes the 'shower,' and here's where we surprise the bride—and the groom—by not giving them a complete set of kitchen equipment. With a mischievous twinkle in our eye, we deposit in front of the happy couple a bushel basket, saying 'The grocer left this a little early for your new home, but you'd better open it now.'" I will take up the story of what is supposed to happen next myself, with a glint of cold horror in my eye.

It seems that the bushel basket is covered with a large piece of brown paper marked with the date of the forthcoming wedding. The very thought of a prospective bridegroom standing in a group of giggling women, with mischievous twinkles in their eyes, and looking at a bushel basket covered with brown paper bearing the date of his wedding is enough to convince anybody that Miss Harriman has got the wrong group of people together. But let us see what happens further (both according to Miss Harriman and according to me). In the basket, she says, are six brown-paper bags. The groom is made to pick up one of these, marked "What the Groom Gets." No groom in the United States would open a bag of that description—he is going through enough the way things are—but let us suppose that he does. Do you know what falls out of it, amid screams of laughter? A peach falls out of it. The bride now picks up a second brown-paper bag, labelled "What the Bride Gets." If you can't picture the look on the face of the groom at this point, I can. Well, out of this bag comes a box of salt marked "Genuine Old Salt." It seems that Miss Harriman has made the groom in this particular case "an ardent fisherman"—hence, Genuine Old Salt. Of course, that wouldn't work in the case of a groom who was not an ardent fisherman. All the guests would just stand there, with their mischievous twinkles turning to puzzled stares. If the groom is *not* an ardent fisherman, Miss Harriman suggests that the bride's bag contain "a gingerbread man cutter." You can hear the pleased roars of the groom and his men friends. "By George," they cry, "this is more fun than a barrel of monkeys!" Everybody is so interested that nobody wonders whether drinks are going to be served, or anything of that sort. There are four brown-paper bags yet to be opened, you see.

The bride now opens the first of these bags, marked simply "The Bride." From this emerge, amid the ecstatic squeals of the ladies, an old potato, a new potato, a borrowed rolling pin, and a blue plum. All the men stare blankly at this array and one of them begins to wonder where they keep the liquor in this house; but the girls explain about the contents of the bag. "Don't you see, Joe? It's 'something old and something new, something borrowed and something blue.'" "What's the potatoes for?" says Joe, gloomily (he is the man who was wondering where they keep the liquor). "I don't get it." "Well, Bert gets it," says the woman who has been explaining to Joe. Bert is a man whose guts Joe hates. "Let him have it," says Joe. This is one of his worst evenings, and there are still three brown-paper bags to be opened. The groom is now holding one of these, on which is printed "The Groom Is In the Kitchen Closet." There is a Bronx cheer from somewhere (probably from Harry Innis) and the groom grins redly; he wishes he were back in college. You and I know that the groom would simply put this bag back in the basket muttering something about it must be getting late, but Miss Harriman says he would open it. All right, he opens it. And pulls out a toy broom. At this point the groom's embarrassment and Joe's gloom are deeper than ever. "What's the idea?" Joe growls. "Stupid!" cries one of the ladies, gaily. "Don't you know 'Here comes the groom, stiff as a groom—stiff as a broom,' I mean?" "No," says Joe. He now moves directly on the pantry to see what there is in the way of drinks around the place. What he finds, in the icebox, is a Mason jar filled with cranberry juice. Joe instantly begins to look for his hat and overcoat, but the hostess captures him. There is more fun to come, she tells him—it is still *frightfully* early, only about eight-thirty.

The hostess leads Joe back to the bushel basket and pulls a fifth bag out of it, which she asks him to open; it is labelled "What the Guests Have." "What's the idea?" Joe grumbles, holding the bag as if it were a doily or a diaper. "Open it, silly!" squeal the excited girls, several of whom, however, are now squealing a little less excitedly than they have been. Joe finally opens the bag and pulls out a box of rice and a box of thyme marked "Good Thyme." "Thyme," mutters Joe, blankly, pronouncing the "h." He hands the boxes to the groom, who distractedly puts them back in the brown bag and puts the brown bag back in the bushel basket. One of the women hastily takes the bag out and opens it again, putting the rice and the thyme on a table. A slight chill falls over the party, on account of the groom's distraction and Joe's sullenness. There is a bad pause, not helped any by Harry Innis's wide yawn, but the hostess quickly hands the sixth and last brown bag to the bride, who extracts from it "a small jar of honey and a moon-shaped cooky-cutter." Joe takes the cooky-cutter from the bride; he is mildly interested for the first time. "What's this thing belong on?" he asks. Somebody takes it away from him. The groom glances at his wristwatch. It is not yet nine o'clock. "Isn't this fun, dear?" asks his bride. "Yeh," says the groom. "Yeh, sure. Swell." The bride realizes, with a quick intuition, that she is losing her hold on the groom. If she is a smart bride, she will be taken suddenly ill at this point and the groom will have to see her home (and Joe will have a chance to cry out with great concern, "Is there any whiskey in the house?"). But let us suppose that the bride is too dumb to realize why she is losing her hold on the groom. The party in this case goes right on. Miss Harriman has a lot more plans for it; she again has a mischievous twinkle in her eye.

The hostess—I shall just call her Miss Harriman—now hands each guest, including Joe, a piece of cardboard ruled off into twenty-five numbered squares (you can look up the article yourself). Each of the squares is large enough for a word to be written in it. Several of the men who have pencils swear they haven't, but Miss Harriman manages to dig up twenty-two pencils and two fountain pens from somewhere. Harry Innis puts his piece of cardboard on the arm of a davenport, stands up, and says, "Whatta you say we all run up to Tim's for a highball?" At this, Joe instantly puts on his overcoat, but one of the women makes him take it off, whispering harshly that he will break Miss Harriman's heart if he doesn't stay. "Aw," says Joe, and slumps into a chair. Mrs. Innis is quietly giving Harry a piece of her mind in a corner.

Miss Harriman now appears before everybody with an *enormous* piece of cardboard, also ruled off into twenty-five squares. Each square contains a dab of some kitchen staple or other: a dab of salt, a dab of pepper, a dab of sugar, a dab of flour, a dab of cayenne, a dab of sage, a dab of cinnamon, a dab of coffee, a dab of tea, a dab of dry mustard, a dab of grated cheese, a dab of baking powder, a dab of cocoa, and dabs of twelve other things. "The bride has her groceries all mixed up!" Miss Harriman sings out brightly. "You must all help her straighten them out! Everybody may look at the things on my cardboard and feel them, too, but nobody must dare taste! Then you write down in the corresponding squares on your own cardboard what you think the different things are!" Most of the men are now standing in a corner talking about the new Buick. One of them has folded his cardboard double and then folded that double and is absently tearing it into strips. Only Bert and two other men stick in the staples game; they identify the salt, sugar, pepper, coffee, and tea, and let it go at that. Ten of the twelve women present get all the answers right. The prize is a can of pepper and, not knowing whom to give it to, Miss Harriman just puts it on a table and claps her hands for attention. She announces that there is another food game to come. "Geezuss," says Joe.

Let Miss Harriman describe the next game in her own words. "In a large pan we gather together as many different vegetables and fruits as we can find—a bunch of carrots, a few beets, a turnip or two, potatoes white and sweet, parsley, lettuce, beans, oranges, grapefruit, pineapple, cherries, bananas— oh, anything. On a tray are placed string, toothpicks, paper towelling, waxed paper, pins, knives, scissors, melon-ball scoops, and any other kitchen implements. This game calls for partners, and as this is a food shower, we try to think of all the foods that seem to go together—Salt and Pepper; Liver and Bacon; Corned Beef and Cabbage; Cream and Sugar, etc. Half the ingredients are written on one color paper, the other on another color, and the guests match them for partners."

If, like Joe (who has drawn Liver and, for partner, a Miss Bacon whom he has been avoiding all evening), you haven't got the idea yet, let me explain. The guests are supposed to manufacture the effigies of brides out of all these materials. Whoever makes the funniest or most original bride wins. (There are a lot of gags at this point, the men guffawing over in their corner. Bill Pierson tells the one about the social worker and the colored woman.) Of this bride-making game Miss Harriman writes: "Loud guffaws and wild dashes to the supply table will result." (She is right about the loud guffaws.) "Imaginations will run riot and hidden talents will come to

the fore." But meanwhile, under cover of the loud guffaws
and the wild dashes, Joe, Harry Innis, and the groom have
slipped out of the house and gone on up to Tim's. When the
bride discovers that the groom has disappeared she is distraught, for she thinks she has lost him for good, and I would
not be surprised if she has.

An appropriate prize for this contest is, according to Miss
Harriman, "a bridal bouquet of scallions and radishes with
streamers of waxed paper, presented as someone plays 'Here
Comes the Bride.'" You can imagine how Joe would have
loved that if he had stayed. But he and Harry Innis and the
groom are on their fifth highball up at Tim's. "And so our
kitchen shower ends," writes Miss Harriman, happily, "with
demands for another wedding as an excuse for more food fun."
You have to admire the woman for whatever it is she has.

22. Goodbye, Mr. O. Charles Meyer!

I AM LEAVING IN A FEW DAYS THE APARTMENT I HAVE LIVED IN for almost a year, on the corner of Eighth Street and Fifth Avenue. Its living-room windows and my bedroom window look out over Eighth Street to the west. Eighth Street is so far below that I cannot make out its signs. The top of a building hides the Jefferson Market clock. All the roofs I see are the same roof; they are indistinguishable, one from another. There is only one thing I shall remember: a sign high up on a building in Eighth Street near Sixth Avenue which says in letters four feet tall, "O. Charles Meyer." Mr. Meyer is in the upholstering business. The sign tells you all about it. I see O. Charles Meyer the first thing every morning when I wake up, and during the day whenever I look out the window, and I go to bed knowing that he is out there, as sturdy and staunch as the little toy soldier. In the months that have gone by, O. Charles Meyer has taken on the semblance of a friend to me. His name is as familiar as the name of any friend I have.

I do not, of course, know O. Charles Meyer in the flesh, but I have a certainty of what he is like, a large, heavy man, elderly and kindly, with the peering eyes of a person who has spent his life puttering with the upholstery of chairs and sofas. In the old chairs and sofas that have been brought to him for reupholstering he has found scissors and penknives and necklaces and unopened letters and hundreds of thousands of dollars in bills which little old ladies have hidden away. If this is not true, I don't want to be told so. O. Charles Meyer is, after all, my own creation. "My O. Charles," I could say of Mr. Meyer as Willa Cather said "My Antonia" of a certain

Turning up with a Green Plush Chair of His Own to Sit in

Miss Shimerda. I figure him as having a number of sons: O. Freddy, O. Samuel, O. George, O. Charles, Jr., and—if it is not too much to ask—O. Henry. I think there may have been three daughters, O. Grace, O. Patience, and O. Charity, but they all married upholsterers in beaver hats and went away, many years ago. I do not want to know what the O. stands for.

I have a sentimental feeling about O. Charles Meyer and I shall hate to leave him, but I am going to have to because my lease is running out and some new tenants will be moving in. I have no other person to turn to of O. Charles Meyer's peculiar stature as an intimate. It will take me a long time to get used to not seeing him in the morning and all day long. One gets sentimentally attached to curious things in this city of steel and cement. In Connecticut, where I used to have a farm, I could look out the window of the room I worked in and see an apple tree, an ancient russet apple tree. I got to know each bend and twist of its branches. It was a friendly and familiar tree, but, like all ancient apple trees, it began to lose its branches; a branch fell off in every storm, so that the appearance of the old tree was always changing. O. Charles Meyer, on the other hand, has always remained the same. O. Charles Meyer is immutable. Eighth Street changes under him in its restless way, people move in and out of the apartments round about, but O. Charles Meyer goes on forever. In such permanence one finds a sense of peace and assurance.

If I ever have to have any upholstering work done, I would want to take it to O. Charles Meyer, but I would be afraid to. I would be afraid that some crisp clerk in the establishment might say to me, "O. Charles Meyer? Why, there is no O. Charles Meyer any longer. Would you like to talk to Mr. Hinkley? Or Mr. Bence?" Something would go out of my life that would make me miserable, if that happened. I would feel that I couldn't trust anything or anybody any more, if O. Charles Meyer let me down. And yet something constantly nags at me—I like to think it's curiosity and not distrust—something nags at me to call up O. Charles on the phone and do something about him. I feel that there is a certain roundness lacking in my association with him. I feel that whereas he has meant a lot to me, I have meant nothing at all to him. I hate to leave my apartment without making a gesture of some kind on his behalf. It has occurred to me to ask him to a cocktail party (I see him turning up with a green plush chair of his own to sit in). I have thought of phrasing my note to him something like this:

"Mr. O. Charles Meyer,

"Eighth Street,

"Dear Mr. Meyer: Will you come to a cocktail party at my apartment tomorrow from 5 to 7? If there is no such person as you, please do not reply." There is a chance here, of course, that Mr. Meyer—or Mr. Hinkley or Mr. Bence—might turn my note over to the police. It would be a nasty bit of evidence in case any suit should ever be filed against me to commit me to an institution. I can hear a lawyer making the most of it. "If it please the Court, I should like to submit in evidence, as State's Exhibit A, this note I hold in my hand. This is a note written by the defendant to one O. Charles Meyer, an upholsterer, inviting Mr. Meyer to a cocktail party. The defendant had never met this man Meyer in his life, as the note proves, and furthermore did not even know whether there *was* such a man. What is more, the note shows that the defendant did not even want to find *out* whether there was such a man. Now, the State contends quite simply . . ."

I suppose, everything considered, that I better drop my relationship with O. Charles Meyer right where it is. The chances are, however, that I will drop around the day before I leave, just to say goodbye and to tell him how much I will miss him, in which case will probably be committed before the summer is out. I'll try not to call on him. I'll try to let it go at this. Goodbye, Mr. O. Charles Meyer! Don't upholster any electric chairs!

23. What Are the Leftists Saying?

For a long time I have had the idea that it would be interesting to attempt to explain to an average worker what the leftist, or socially conscious, literary critics are trying to say. Since these critics are essentially concerned with the improvement of the worker's status, it seems fitting and proper that the worker should be educated in the meaning of their pronouncements. The critics themselves believe, of course, in the education of the worker, but they are divided into two schools about it: those who believe the worker should be taught beforehand why there must be a revolution, and those who believe that he should be taught afterward why there was one. This is but one of many two-school systems which divide the leftist intellectuals and keep them so busy in controversy that the worker is pretty much left out of things. It is my plan to escort a worker to a hypothetical, but typical, gathering of leftist literary critics and interpret for him, insofar as I can, what is being said there. The worker is likely to be so confused at first, and so neglected, that he will want to slip out and go to Minsky's; but it is important that he stay, and I hope that he has already taken a chair and removed his hat. I shall sit beside him and try to clarify what is going on.

Nothing, I must explain while we are waiting for the gentlemen to gather, is going to be easy. This is partly because it is a primary tenet of leftist criticism to avoid what is known as Oversimplification. This is a word our worker is going to encounter frequently at the gathering of critics and it is important that he understand what it means. Let me get at it by quoting a sentence from a recent review in *The Nation* by a socially conscious critic: "In so far as men assert and

The Others Are Not so Much Listening as Waiting for an Opening

counter-assert, you can draw an assertion from the comparison of their assertions." As it stands, that is not oversimplified, because no one can point to any exact or absolute meaning it has. Now I will oversimplify it. A says, "Babe Ruth is dead" (assertion). B says, "Babe Ruth is alive" (counter-assertion). C says, "You guys seem to disagree" (assertion drawn from comparison of assertions). Here I have brought the critic's sentence down to a definite meaning by providing a concrete instance. Leftist criticism does not believe in that, contending that all thought is in a state of motion, and that in every thought there exists simultaneously "being," "non-being," and "becoming," and that in the end every thought disappears by being absorbed into its opposite. I am afraid that I am over-simplifying again.

Let us get back to our meeting. About sixteen leftist literary critics have now gathered in the room. Several are talking and the others are not so much listening as waiting for an opening. Let us cock an ear toward Mr. Hubert Camberwell. Mr. Camberwell is saying, "Sinclair Lewis has dramatized the process of disintegration, as well as his own dilemma, in the outlines of his novels, in the progress of his characters, and sometimes, and most painfully, in the lapses of taste and precision that periodically weaken the structure of his prose." This is a typical leftist critic's sentence. It has a facile, portentous swing, it damns a prominent author to hell, and it covers a tremendous amount of ground. It also has an air of authority, and because of this the other critics will attack it. Up speaks a Mr. Scholzweig: "But you cannot, with lapses of any kind, *dramatize* a process, you can only *annotate* it." This is a minor criticism, at best, but it is the only one Mr. Scholzweig can think of, because he agrees in general with what has been said about Sinclair Lewis (whose books he has never been able to read). At this point Donald Crowley announces that as yet nobody has *defined* anything; that is, nobody has defined "lapses," "dramatize," "process," or "annotate." While a small, excited man in shell-rim glasses is asking him how he would define the word "definition" in a world of flux, let us listen to Mr. Herman Bernheim. Mr. Bernheim is muttering something about Camberwell's "methodology" and his failure to "implement" his argument. Now, "methodology," as the leftist intellectuals use it, means any given wrong method of approach to a subject. "To implement" means (1) to have at the tip of one's tongue everything that has been written by any leftist since Marx, for the purpose of denying it, and (2) to possess and make use of historical references that begin like this: "Because of the more solidly articulated structure of French society, the deep-seated sentiments and prejudices of the northern French, and the greater geographical and political accessibility of France to the propaganda of the counter-Reformation," etc., etc.

The critics have by this time got pretty far away from Camberwell's analysis of Sinclair Lewis, but this is the customary procedure when leftists begin refuting one another's statements, and is one phase of what is known as "dialectic." Dialectic, in this instance, means the process of discriminating one's own truth from the other person's error. This leads to "factionalism," another word our worker must be familiar with. Factionalism is that process of disputation by means of which the main point at issue is lost sight of. Now, the main point at issue here—namely, the analysis of Sinclair Lewis—becomes even more blurred by the fact that a critic named Kyle Forsythe, who has just come into the room, gets the erroneous notion that everybody is discussing Upton Sinclair. He begins, although it is not at all relevant, to talk about "escapism." Escapism means the activities of anyone who is not a leftist critic or writer. The discussion, to our worker, will now appear to get so far out of hand that we must bring him a Scotch-and-soda if we are to hold his interest much longer. He will probably want to know whether one leftist intellectual ever agrees with another, and, under cover of the loud talking, I shall explain the one form of agreement which these critics have. I call it the "that he—but when" form of agreement. Let us say that one leftist critic writes in a liberal weekly as follows: "I like poetry, but I don't like Tennyson." Another leftist critic will write often in the same issue and immediately following the first one's article: "That he likes poetry, we must concede Mr. Blank, but when he says that Tennyson is a great poet, we can only conclude that he does not like poetry at all." This is, of course, greatly oversimplified.

Midnight eventually arrives at our party and everybody begins "unmasking" everybody else's "ideology." To explain what unmasking an ideology means, I must give an example. Suppose that I were to say to one of the critics at this party, "My country, 'tis of thee, sweet land of liberty." He would unmask my ideology—that is expose the background of my illusion—by pointing out that I am the son of wealthy bourgeois parents who employed an English butler. This is not true, but my ideology would be unmasked, anyway. It is interesting to note that it takes only one leftist critic to expose anybody's ideology, and that every leftist critic unmasks ideologies in his own special way. In this sense, Marxist criticism is very similar to psychoanalysis. Ideology-unmasking is a great deal like dream interpretation and leads to just as many mystic results.

A general midnight unmasking of ideologies at a gathering of leftist literary critics is pretty exciting, and I hope that a second Scotch-and-soda will persuade our worker to stay. If he does, he will find out that when your ideology is unmasked, you can't do anything with it, because it has no "social currency." In other words, anything that you say or do will have no more validity than Confederate money.

The party now breaks up, without ill feeling, because the critics have all had such a good time at the unmasking. A leftist critic gets as much fun out of disputation, denial, and disparagement as a spaniel puppy gets out of a steak bone. Each one will leave, confident that he has put each of the others in his place and that they realize it. This is known as the "united front." On our way out, however, I must explain to the worker the meaning of an extremely important term in Marxist criticism; namely, "Dialectical Materialism." Dialectical Materialism, then, is based on two fundamental laws of dialectics: the law of the permeation of opposites, or polar unity, and the law of the negation of the negation, or development through opposites. This second proposition is the basic law of all processes of thought. I will first state the law itself and then support it with examples . . . Hey, worker! Wait for baby!

24. How to Write an Autobiography

THE COMMUNIST INTELLECTUALS KNOW A LOT MORE THAN I do, and while I am the first, or among the first, anyway, to admit it, I am also the first to explain why. For one thing, they keep all the letters they get from intellectual friends and use them in their writings; and, for another thing, they keep carbon copies of all the letters they write. Everybody gets off a few pretty good cracks, comments, and the like in his letters, but almost everybody forgets them after he sends them off. I suspect there is a type of author (both Communist and bourgeois) who, dashing off, in a letter, a sentence or a paragraph, or even a phrase, he thinks is pretty good, copies it down before he mails the letter. But the Communist intellectuals, as I say, keep carbon copies of the whole works. This seems to me unfair, for some reason; maybe I don't mean unfair, maybe I mean something else, but if I do, I mean something I don't like.

Take "An American Testament," published not long ago. It was written by one of America's brightest Communist intellectuals, Mr. Joseph Freeman. It runs, I have estimated, to 330,000 words. I can't go back through the book and find all the letters Mr. Freeman quotes, and I doubt if he could, but I can find some of them. On page 191, for instance, there is a paragraph beginning: " 'For me personally'—Irwin [Edman]

wrote me from Dresden in the fall of 1920—'the world these last few weeks has been almost romantically perfect. I have been moving, to quote your own phrase, through rich experiences, though not swiftly; not swiftly because the experiences have been too rich to hurry through.'" The letter, or the part of it that is quoted, runs to about three hundred words. It is followed by a thousand-word letter Mr. Freeman wrote to Mr. Edman in answer to his, and at the end of that Mr. Freeman writes: "To this long disquisition, Irwin replied from Venice three days later"—and there follow five hundred words of that. Then comes part of a long letter from Irwin in Rome. This is followed by a letter from Louis Smith, and that is followed by Mr. Freeman's answer, and *that* is followed by a letter from "Mac's sister-in-law Lillian," and then comes Mr. Freeman's answer to her, and then a long letter he wrote to Professor James Harvey Robinson, to which Professor Robinson did not reply (if he had, I know darn well the letter would have been printed, together with Mr. Freeman's answer to it). All these letters were written seventeen years ago, but there they are.

Now, whether or not these letters are interesting or important is beside the point I want to make, but I suppose it is only fair to give some idea of what they are like. Take the opening sentence of Mr. Freeman's thousand-word letter to Mr. Edman. He wrote: "It was my idealistic, religious, artistic bias which made me blind to pragmatism." That is the topic sentence of a letter which somehow does not sound like a letter to a friend at all. It sounds more like an essay written to save in a file and someday print in a book. You get the inescapable feeling that the original was sent to a friend in order to get a well-written essay in return, which also could be used in the book. That, of course, is one way to get a book together, and the fact that it is not my way is not so

much because I don't like the studied and disingenuous tone
of the whole thing as because I could never keep a carbon
copy or a letter for fifteen or twenty years, the way Mr.
Freeman can. If I keep a letter two weeks, I am doing fine.
Then, too, my friends never write me long letters dealing with
profound subjects. Their letters are usually hurried and to the
point, and they sometimes deal with matters which I wouldn't
want to have exposed in a book even after I was dead.

Mr. Irwin Edman and some of Mr. Freeman's other corre-
spondents are well-known writers, and whereas I have got a
few letters from well-known writers in my time, none of them
would be usable in a book even if I could find them. Some
of them are both illegible and illiterate, as if they had been
written at a bar. Few of them say anything, really, that anybody would want to read, and none of them sounds as if it
had been rewritten several times, the way Mr. Freeman's
letters to his friends, and theirs to him, sound. Communist
intellectuals are the most facile and articulate of all writers,
and words come out of most of them like water from a faucet,
so I can't say for sure the letters were rewritten; I just say
they sound rewritten. (Rewriting a letter to a girl is all right,
under certain circumstances, but that's as far as I will go.)

I happen to remember a letter one well-known writer sent
to me some years ago, because it contained only one sentence.
It read: "Will you please for God's sake come back with my
shoes?" That's all; just that one sentence. And I wouldn't
have got that if he had been able to get me on the phone. It
seems that this author and myself and a couple of lecturers
from Hollywood went to the author's apartment one night.
Around five o'clock in the morning, the argument on idealism,
religion, art, and pragmatism having rather worn me out, I
took off my shoes and lay down on the author's bed. When
I got up, I put on his shoes by mistake—not the ones he had

on, of course, although I could have done that, but another
pair, apparently his favorites. I noticed on my way home that
I couldn't walk very well—my feet hurt—but I put it down
to the argument. The next morning, however, I had a terrible
time getting the shoes on. They were two sizes too small
for me, but since I thought they were my own, I could only
believe that my feet had swelled. I started to walk up Fifth
Avenue, with the gait of a man who is stalking a bird across
wet cement. It was pretty painful, and I finally had to take a
cab. I suffered all day, but the next morning the author's letter
came in asking me to bring back his shoes, and you can
imagine my relief, both physical and mental. I had been
on the point of going to a doctor. None of this really belongs
in a book.

Such letters as I get from persons other than friends of
mine are usually written with pen and ink, and often on
blue or purple paper. These are almost impossible to make
out, and I couldn't use them in a book even if I wanted to.
I have one at hand now, for instance, which came just a day
or two ago and hasn't been lost yet. I'll quote the first few
lines the way I make them out (the letter is written in black
India ink on aquamarine paper):

DEAR MR. THUMBER:
   For agree blest you've been out of my perine parasites. The obline
being in case you're interested, a girl whose name escapes me, but merits
swell pecul, and I know you'd know who she is.

That's all I can get out of that. It appears to be signed
Keriumiy Luud Roosool, or Kaasaat. Nothing, of course,
could be done with it. Even when I can decipher all but a
word or two of my correspondence (I never get *every* word),
nothing much can be done with it. For instance, I got a postcard last January from a famous man in Washington, and

although I practically mastered it, I don't see how I could ever work it into a book. I will quote it verbatim:

WASHINGTON, D. C.
JAN. 8, 1937

MR. JAMES THURBER—On reading some back numbers of N. Yorker came across article, "An Outline of Science." It is plain you know a thing or two about science, but—heh! heh! heh! heh!—[illegible word]. Especially speed of light & those terrible bloodhounds.

Yours Truly, ALBERT GAMBLE,
Hobo Scientist

(Originator of famous Fireball-Waterball Theory of Swimming Continents.)

I'm afraid I'm not going to be able to use any letters or other communications in my own 300,000-word testament, unless I make up some—and I didn't make up Mr. Gamble's— or sneak a few out of Mr. Freeman's book. He'd probably never miss them.

25. After the Steppe Cat, What?

THERE ARE MANY SIGNS WHICH INDICATE THAT OUR CIVILIZA-tion is on the wane, and these are to be seen not only in the economic, political, and military phenomena of our dying day, which are portentously analyzed in every periodical one picks up, but also in a tiny phenomenon here, a small paragraph there. Poets have a quick eye to detect these minute portents of the approaching end. The clairvoyant Stephen Vincent Benét was probably just one step ahead of actuality when he wrote of observing a termite which held in its tiny jaws a glittering crumb of steel. Morris Bishop, another seer who views tomorrow clearly, has written of the time when in the mothproof closet will dwell the moth.

It is all very interesting to indulge in polysyllabic discussions of dialectical materialism and dialectical idealism, of democracy and the totalitarian state, of Marxist hope and capitalist illusion, but I am more interested in wondering whether the fleck of dust that got in my eye yesterday may not have been all that was left of a planet like ours which burned out a million years ago, ten hundred billion miles away. Perhaps I was struck with that wonder because once in Carthage, two thousand years ago, the gleam of a Roman shield got in my eye or a speck of that sand which was to conquer the very conquerors of one of the oldest and strongest civilizations

known to man. A bit of steel glittering here, a moth fluttering there, a handful of dust in the air: these are the signs of
doom.

Perhaps some manifestations of the sort always accompany
any politico-social collapse. Then again, who is there to say
for sure that political and social collapse doesn't merely accompany such manifestations? Which reached Rome first, the

The Aardvark

Visigoth or the wolf? It is a momentous question, calling
for a great amount of research, and I am sorry I haven't got
space to pursue it. I have space for only a few random notes on
this general theme, which may haply lead some scientist—or
some poet—to a more exhaustive treatment of the subject.

Let us look, first, at a paragraph in the *New York Times*,
not long ago, by its Berlin correspondent, Mr. Otto D.
Tolischus.

This winter's extraordinary character is already arousing concern for
this year's crops; and in addition, certain districts, especially Silesia,

complain of a veritable plague of rats and mice. German agricultural quarters are now engaged in a hot public debate regarding charges that the many draining, land reclamation, and river regulation projects the National Socialist regime has undertaken are so interfering with the country's water economy as to turn Germany gradually into a steppe. There are assertions by experts that certain unmistakable steppe animals and plants are already beginning to make themselves at home in Germany.

Here we see how the Nazi land-reclamation engineers are beginning to make Germany into a steppe, exactly as the United States' land-*wasting* pioneers began to make this country into a Sahara. There would appear to be no way

The Bandicoot

out, in a time of world decay, no matter what you do. It proceeds by curious, inexorable laws of its own, this ending of a jaded civilization, that a new way of life may begin. Nature helps along the destruction by sending her rodents in hordes to gnaw at the very foundations of man's existence. Thus rats and mice appear in Silesia—and don't get one hundredth the attention that LaGuardia got when he gnawed only at German pride. And yet these rodents are a hundred times more important, for they will outlast LaGuardia—and

German pride, too—as the mollusks from which Tyrian dye was made have outlived Tyre and the Tyrians.

The desert into which America is turning is perhaps more familiar than the steppe into which Germany is changing. A steppe is a large tract of arid land characterized by xerophilous vegetation—that is, plant life that can stand the absence or scarcity of moisture. It is a primitive sort of land, flat and treeless, suitable for open warfare, fit for man and his activities in the last stages of a civilization. Among the "unmistakable steppe animals" that will eventually trot into Berlin is the steppe cat, a small wildcat. It has grayish-white fur, useful as camouflage in the open spaces, but it is interesting to note that

The Wombat

it also has blackish transverse bands, a coloration obviously developed by nature to serve as camouflage when it finally reaches the cities, where it can creep unnoticed between car tracks and behind picket fences.

Walter Lippman recently insisted in the *Atlantic Monthly*

that "Communism and fascism are not only much alike as systems of government; they are alike in the inwardness of their purpose." To which I feel impelled to add that the systems and purposes of man are all one to the steppe cat. And to the termite, the rat, the mouse, the grasshopper, the locust, the caterpillar, the weevil, the wombat, the rabbit, the aardvark, the bandicoot, the Scotch terrier, the cockroach, the coddling moth, and the Colorado potato beetle, to name just a few of the thousands of insects and animals that will go to town with the steppe cat when the Great Invasion begins.

In the olden days, of which Omar sang, it was the lion and the lizard that moved sleepily into the courtyard of the

The Steppe Cat

palace; they had no system and no purpose, so that man, rising again from the ashes of his ruined civilization, could easily oust them. The next and greatest invasion of the lower species will find, I think, all the living things, with a kind of planned economy, moving in on man, who has too long been keeping a hostile and fearful eye on his fellow man, to the exclusion of any interest in the steppe cat and the steppe cat's million allies. Pick up any large dictionary and turn the pages —you'll have to turn only one or two—till you come to the picture of a pest of some sort. In the majority of cases you will find under its name these descriptive phrases: "now widely distributed" and "often causing great damage." There is a bug that works at the foundation of houses; there is one that destroys each kind of tree; there is one that gets into tea and spices; there is one that specializes in the ruining of tobacco; there is even one, common to the Congo, that seeks to inhabit the human eye.

Working quietly through the ages, the insects and the rodents, at once specialists and collectivists, have prepared themselves, I believe, to take over the world. I see no reason to believe that they will not make a better job of it than man. One July day in 1863 a handful of troopers rode idly into a town called Gettysburg, in Pennsylvania. The inhabitants glanced at them and went about their business. There could be no war in that little town; the troopers would ride away. Two or three steppe cats are observed in Germany, and the fact is recorded briefly on page 8 of the *New York Times*.

Not long ago Dr. Earnest A. Hooton, Harvard professor of anthropology and President of the American Association of Physical Anthropologists, announced in a lecture that man is deteriorating—in behavior, in physique, and in intelligence. This was not news to those of us who have our ears to the steppe. I think it also quite probable that it was not news to the steppe cat. In the course of his talk Dr. Hooton pointed out that man has not added any new domestic animals to his collection since the time when animals were first put to use. He might have extended this observation to include the prophecy that one day the animals may begin, in their own way, to domesticate man, who, as Dr. Hooton said, is becoming ludicrous in body, ineffective in culture, and moronic in intelligence. In short, a set-up for animals, which are becoming less ludicrous, more cunning, and smarter every year.

Dr. Hooton also said that man is "not yet successful in his fight against micro-organisms, to any great extent." To which he might have added that, while man is peering into microscopes at micro-organisms, the steppe cat has slipped into Germany. It was not so long ago that the praying mantis came in a horde to look over New York City. You could find them reconnoitering high up on the Empire State Building. They peered into bedrooms and kitchens from window sills. They were all over the place. Then they quietly went away. The papers and the public treated it as a curious but unimportant phenomenon, that visit. I regard it as an extremely significant occurrence. Scouting planes in advance of the infantry, the tanks, and the bombers.

Where Carthage once stood in her glory and pride there rises a cluster of modern villas, forming a suburb of the modern city of Tunis. Thus has the greatness of a sovereign power diminished. To what new kind of metropolis may Tunis someday become a suburb? Look through your field glasses at the nearest steppe land—look close to the ground. There—see that grayish-white blur, with the blackish transverse bands?

26. Women Go On Forever

THE OUTLOOK FOR THE CONTINUANCE OF THE LIFE OF MAN ON this earth, in the style to which he has been accustomed, is, as everybody must surely know, not very bright. Socially, economically, physically and intellectually, Man is slowly going, I am reliably informed, to hell. His world is blowing over; his day is done. I have the word of a hundred scientists and psychologists for this sorry fact. You have but to pick up the nearest book or magazine—or the one right next to it— to read the disconcerting news.

There have been prophecies of doom, such as Oswald Spengler's; there have been diagnoses of the malady, such as Dr. Carrel's; there have been programs for its correction, such as Karl Marx's; there have been sociological formulas for its clarification, such as Pareto's; there have even been whole new cosmogonies proposed, such as H. G. Wells'. Each expert, in his fashion, has analyzed the decline of Mankind and most of them have prescribed remedies for the patient. But none of them, I believe, has detected the fact that although Man, as he is now traveling, is headed for extinction, Woman is not going with him. It is, I think, high time to abandon the loose generic term "Man," for it is no longer logically inclusive or scientifically exact. There is Man and there is Woman, and Woman is going her own way.

Scientists, statisticians, actuaries, all those men who place numbers above hunches, figures above feelings, facts above possibilities, the normal above the phenomenal, will tell you that the life span of the average man is, and will remain, approximately the same as the life span of the average woman. This is because, with their eyes on the average, they fail to discern the significant. The significant is never, to begin with, larger than a man's hand, and sometimes it is no larger than a hole in a dike—or a three-line item in the New York *Times*.

It was on January 14, 1937, that I clipped this bit of significance from the pages of that newspaper: "La Salle, Ont.—Cheerful, remarkably agile, Mrs. Felice Meloche celebrated her 104th birthday here yesterday. Mrs. Meloche sang for her guests the French song 'Alouette' without a quaver in her voice."

Since that day I have kept track of news items dealing with persons who have lived to be 100 years old or older, and the record is provocative. It contains the names of six men. Four of them were written about because they had died. The oldest of the six was 103. The record contains the names of 37 women. Twenty-four of the items, or about two-thirds, reported how the ladies celebrated their birthdays—by singing, dancing, riding in airplanes, playing kettledrums, running foot races, chinning themselves or entertaining their great-great-grandchildren. Let us look at the record for one week, the last week in March—a record that is confined, because of the short scope of my news sources, to greater New York and the region roundabout:

On March 25, Mrs. Amorette E. Fraser of Brooklyn celebrated her 101st birthday by taking a vigorous walk, riding in a taxi, standing for two hours to greet dozens of visitors, and denouncing the Roosevelt Administration. On March 28, Mrs. Emily S. Andrews, of Plainfield, New Jersey, celebrated her 101st birthday by entertaining 100 guests at tea—an event which she took in her stride. On March 29, the Burlington County Almshouse in New Jersey was destroyed by fire and among those saved was "Uncle Joe" Willow, aged 103. As reporters gathered around and were about to interview this remarkable ancient, who should emerge casually from the flames, fit as a fiddle and chipper as a lark, but "Aunt Mary" Asay, aged 114? When Joe Willow was ten years old and in the fourth grade, Mary Asay was 21—and probably married and running a big household. "The fire," said the story in the New York *Herald Tribune,* "was discovered by a 132-year-old-nurse"—no, I'm wrong there. It was discovered by a nurse in the 132-year-old east wing of the building. But anyway, here was Mary Asay, born when James Monroe was President, one of the numerous outstanding proofs of my theory that women are tending to become immortal, that the day will come when they will never die. They are flourishing on all sides of us, singing and dancing and denouncing the Administration, these deathless ladies, some of whom have outlived their husbands by periods ranging from 50 to 100 years.

The increasingly tenacious hold on life of the female of the human species begins, my researches show, at birth. I recently asked an eminent obstetrician whether, if a baby he was about to deliver were in foetal distress, he would prefer it to be a boy or a girl. Prefacing his hesitant answer with the cautious announcement that there are no scientific data to go by, he said he would prefer it to be a girl. Does any obstetrician, I asked him, believe for a moment that five *males* would have survived up there in Callander, Ontario, on that historic night? To which, since, again lacking data, he declined to reply, I replied for him; no. The birth of five females and their survival against incredible odds assumes the clear nature of a portent that only the Scientist is too blind to see. Man's day is indeed done; the epoch of Woman is upon us.

I should like in conclusion to call attention to figures I and

II which accompany this treatise and which you probably thought I had forgotten. They are, you will observe, absolutely identical faces, save that one (Fig. I) is male and the other (Fig. II) is female. Yet it is easy to discern in the male physiognomy the symptoms of that extinction which threatens his sex: an air of uncertainty, an expression of futility, a general absence of "hold," which are inescapable.

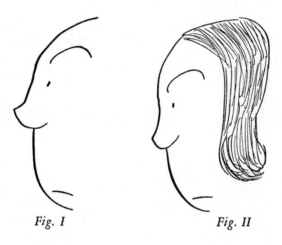

Fig. I   *Fig. II*

There is about the female, on the other hand, a hint of survival, a threat of perpetuation, a general "Here I am and here I always will be," which are equally unmistakable. The male is obviously not looking at anything; he is lost in the moody contemplation of an existence which is slipping away from him; already its outlines are far and vague. The female unquestionably has her eyes on an objective; you can feel the solid, sharp edges of her purpose.

It was, unless I've got my notes mixed up, our old friend Professor Ernest A. Hooton of Harvard who, in the course of a recent lecture on the physical and mental decline of Mankind, observed that "when women reach a certain age they seem to become immortal." I think that he and I have got hold of something. Just what good it will do us, being males, I do not know.

27. The Wood Duck

M R. KREPP, OUR VEGETABLE MAN, HAD TOLD US WE MIGHT find some cider out the New Milford road a way—we would come to a sign saying "Morris Plains Farm" and that would be the place. So we got into the car and drove down the concrete New Milford road, which is black in the center with the dropped oil of a million cars. It's a main-trunk highway; you can go fifty miles an hour on it except where warning signs limit you to forty or, near towns, thirty-five, but nobody ever pays any attention to these signs. Even then, in November, dozens of cars flashed past us with a high, ominous whine, their tires roaring rubberly on the concrete. We found Morris Plains Farm without any trouble. There was a big white house to the left of the highway; only a few yards off the road a small barn had been made into a roadside stand, with a dirt driveway curving up to the front of it. A spare, red-cheeked man stood in the midst of baskets and barrels of red apples and glass jugs of red cider. He was waiting on a man and a woman. I turned into the driveway—and put the brakes on hard. I had seen, just in time, a duck.

It was a small, trim duck, and even I, who know nothing about wild fowl, knew that this was no barnyard duck, this was a wild duck. He was all alone. There was no other bird of any kind around, not even a chicken. He was immensely solitary. With none of the awkward waddling of a domestic duck, he kept walking busily around in the driveway, now and then billing up water from a dirty puddle in the middle of

the drive. His obvious contentment, his apparently perfect
adjustment to his surroundings, struck me as something of a
marvel. I got out of the car and spoke about it to a man
who had driven up behind me in a rattly sedan. He wore a
leather jacket and high, hard boots, and I figured he would
know what kind of duck this was. He did. "That's a wood
duck," he said. "It dropped in here about two weeks ago,
Len says, and's been here ever since."

The proprietor of the stand, in whose direction my inform-
ant had nodded as he spoke, helped his customers load a
basket of apples into their car and walked over to us. The

duck stepped, with a little flutter of its wings, into the dirty
puddle, took a small, unconcerned swim, and got out again,
ruffling its feathers. "It's rather an odd place for a wood duck,
isn't it?" asked my wife. Len grinned and nodded; we all
watched the duck. "He's a banded duck," said Len. "There's
a band on his leg. The state game commission sends out a
lot of 'em. This'n lighted here two weeks ago—it was on a
Saturday—and he's been around ever since." "It's funny he
wouldn't be frightened away, with all the cars going by and
all the people driving in," I said. Len chuckled. "He seems
to like it here," he said. The duck wandered over to some
sparse grass at the edge of the road, aimlessly, but with an
air of settled satisfaction. "He's tame as anything," said Len. "I
guess they get tame when them fellows band 'em." The man in

the leather jacket said, " 'Course they haven't let you shoot wood duck for a long while and that might make 'em tame, too." "Still," said my wife (we forgot about the cider for the moment), "it's strange he would stay here, right on the road almost." "Sometimes," said Len, reflectively, "he goes round back o' the barn. But mostly he's here in the drive." "But don't they," she asked, "let them loose in the woods after they're banded? I mean, aren't they supposed to stock up the forests?" "I guess they're supposed to," said Len, chuckling again. "But 'pears this'n didn't want to."

An old Ford truck lurched into the driveway and two men in the seat hailed the proprietor. They were hunters, big, warmly dressed, heavily shod men. In the back of the truck was a large bird dog. He was an old pointer and he wore an expression of remote disdain for the world of roadside commerce. He took no notice of the duck. The two hunters said something to Len about cider, and I was just about to chime in with my order when the accident happened. A car went by the stand at fifty miles an hour, leaving something scurrying in its wake. It was the duck, turning over and over on the concrete. He turned over and over swiftly, but lifelessly, like a thrown feather duster, and then he lay still. "My God," I cried, "they've killed your duck, Len!" The accident gave me a quick feeling of anguished intimacy with the bereaved man. "Oh, now," he wailed. "Now, that's awful!" None of us for a moment moved. Then the two hunters walked toward the road, slowly, self-consciously, a little embarrassed in the face of this quick incongruous ending of a wild fowl's life in the middle of a concrete highway. The pointer stood up, looked after the hunters, raised his ears briefly, and then lay down again.

It was the man in the leather jacket finally who walked out to the duck and tried to pick it up. As he did so, the duck stood up. He looked about him like a person who has been abruptly wakened and doesn't know where he is. He didn't ruffle his feathers. "Oh, he isn't quite *dead!*" said my wife. I knew how she felt. We were going to have to see the duck die; somebody would have to kill him, finish him off. Len stood beside us. My wife took hold of his arm. The man in the leather jacket knelt down, stretched out a hand, and the duck moved slightly away. Just then, out from behind the barn, limped a setter dog, a lean white setter dog with black spots. His right back leg was useless and he kept it off the ground. He stopped when he saw the duck in the road and gave it a point, putting his head out, lifting his left front leg, maintaining a wavering, marvellous balance on two legs. He was like a drunken man drawing a bead with a gun. This new menace, this anticlimax, was too much. I think I yelled.

What happened next happened as fast as the automobile accident. The setter made his run, a limping, wobbly run, and he was in between the men and the bird before they saw him. The duck flew, got somehow off the ground a foot or two, and tumbled into the grass of the field across the road, the dog after him. It seemed crazy, but the duck could fly—a little, anyway. "Here, here," said Len, weakly. The hunters shouted, I shouted, my wife screamed, "He'll kill him! He'll *kill* him!" The duck flew a few yards again, the dog at his tail. The dog's third plunge brought his nose almost to the duck's tail, and then one of the hunters tackled the animal and pulled him down and knelt in the grass, holding him. We all breathed easier. My wife let go Len's arm.

Len started across the road after the duck, who was fluttering slowly, waveringly, but with a definite purpose, toward a wood that fringed the far side of the field. The bird was dazed, but a sure, atavistic urge was guiding him; he was going home. One of the hunters joined Len in his pursuit.

The other came back across the road, dragging the indignant setter; the man in the leather jacket walked beside them. We all watched Len and his companion reach the edge of the wood and stand there, looking; they had followed the duck through the grass slowly, so as not to alarm him; he had been alarmed enough. "He'll never come back," said my wife. Len and the hunter finally turned and came back through the grass. The duck had got away from them. We walked out to meet them at the edge of the concrete. Cars began to whiz by in both directions. I realized, with wonder, that all the time the duck, and the hunters, and the setter were milling around in the road, not one had passed. It was as if traffic had been held up so that our little drama could go on. "He couldn't o' been much hurt," said Len. "Likely just grazed and pulled along in the wind of the car. Them fellows don't look out for anything. It's a sin." My wife had a question for him. "Does your dog always chase the duck?" she asked. "Oh, that ain't my dog," said Len. "He just comes around." The hunter who had been holding the setter now let him go, and he slunk away. The pointer, I noticed, lay with his eyes closed. "But doesn't the duck mind the dog?" persisted my wife. "Oh, he minds him," said Len. "But the dog's never really hurt him none yet. There's always somebody around."

We drove away with a great deal to talk about (I almost forgot the cider). I explained the irony, I think I explained the profound symbolism, of a wild duck's becoming attached to a roadside stand. My wife strove simply to understand the duck's viewpoint. She didn't get anywhere. I knew even then, in the back of my mind, what would happen. We decided, after a cocktail, to drive back to the place and find out if the duck had returned. My wife hoped it wouldn't be there, on account of the life it led in the driveway; I hoped it wouldn't because I felt that would be, somehow, too pat an ending. Night was falling when we started off again for Morris Plains Farm. It was a five-mile drive and I had to put my bright lights on before we got there. The barn door was closed for the night. We didn't see the duck anywhere. The only thing to do was to go up to the house and inquire. I knocked on the door and a young man opened it. "Is—is the proprietor here?" I asked. He said no, he had gone to Waterbury. "We wanted to know," my wife said, "whether the duck came back." "What?" he asked, a little startled, I thought. Then, "Oh, the duck. I saw him around the driveway when my father drove off." He stared at us, waiting. I thanked him and started back to the car. My wife lingered, explaining, for a moment. "He thinks we're crazy," she said, when she got into the car. We drove on a little distance. "Well," I said, "he's back." "I'm glad he is, in a way," said my wife. "I hated to think of him all alone out there in the woods."

28. The Admiral on the Wheel

WHEN THE COLORED MAID STEPPED ON MY GLASSES THE other morning, it was the first time they had been broken since the late Thomas A. Edison's seventy-ninth birthday. I remember that day well, because I was working for a newspaper then and I had been assigned to go over to West Orange that morning and interview Mr. Edison. I got up early and, in reaching for my glasses under the bed (where I always put them), I found that one of my more sober and reflective Scotch terriers was quietly chewing them. Both tortoiseshell temples (the pieces that go over your ears) had been eaten and Jeannie was toying with the lenses in a sort of jaded way. It was in going over to Jersey that day, without my glasses, that I realized that the disadvantages of defective vision (bad eyesight) are at least partially compensated for by its peculiar advantages. Up to that time I had been in the habit of going to bed when my glasses were broken and lying there until they were fixed again. I had believed I could not go very far without them, not more than a block, anyway, on account of the danger of bumping into things, getting a headache, losing my way. None of those things happened, but a lot of others did. I saw the Cuban flag flying over a national bank, I saw a gay old lady with a gray parasol walk right through the side of a truck, I saw a cat roll across a street in a small striped barrel, I saw bridges rise lazily into the air, like balloons.

I suppose you have to have just the right proportion of sight to encounter such phenomena: I seem to remember that oculists have told me I have only two-fifths vision without what one of them referred to as "artificial compensation" (glasses). With three-fifths vision or better, I suppose the

Cuban flag would have been an American flag, the gay old lady a garbage man with a garbage can on his back, the cat a piece of butcher's paper blowing in the wind, the floating bridges smoke from tugs, hanging in the air. With perfect vision, one is extricably trapped in the workaday world, a prisoner of reality, as lost in the commonplace America of 1937 as Alexander Selkirk was lost on his lonely island. For the hawk-eyed person life has none of those soft edges which for me blur into fantasy; for such a person an electric welder is merely an electric welder, not a radiant fool setting off a sky-rocket by day. The kingdom of the partly blind is a little like

Oz, a little like Wonderland, a little like Poictesme. Anything you can think of, and a lot you never would think of, can happen there.

For three days after the maid, in cleaning the apartment, stepped on my glasses—I had not put them far enough under the bed—I worked at home and did not go uptown to have them fixed. It was in this period that I made the acquaintance of a remarkable Chesapeake spaniel. I looked out my window and after a moment spotted him, a noble, silent dog lying on a ledge above the entrance to a brownstone house in lower Fifth Avenue. He lay there, proud and austere, for three days and nights, sleepless, never eating, the perfect watchdog. No ordinary dog could have got up on the high ledge above the doorway, to begin with; no ordinary people would have owned such an animal. The ordinary people were the people who walked by the house and did not see the dog. Oh, I got my glasses fixed finally and I know that now the dog has gone, but I haven't looked to see what prosaic object occupies the spot where he so staunchly stood guard over one of the last of the old New York houses on Fifth Avenue; perhaps an unpainted flowerbox or a cleaning cloth dropped from an upper window by a careless menial. The moment of disenchantment would be too hard; I never look out that particular window any more.

Sometimes at night, even with my glasses on, I see strange and unbelievable sights, mainly when I am riding in an automobile which somebody else is driving (I never drive myself at night out of fear that I might turn up at the portals of some mystical monastery and never return). Only last summer I was riding with someone along a country road when suddenly I cried at him to look out. He slowed down and asked me sharply what was the matter. There is no worse experience than to have someone shout at you to look out for something you don't see. What this driver didn't see and I did see (two-fifths vision works a kind of magic in the night) was a little old admiral in full-dress uniform riding a bicycle at right angles to the car I was in. He might have been starlight behind a tree, or a billboard advertising Moxie; I don't know —we were quickly past the place he rode out of; but I would recognize him if I saw him again. His beard was blowing in the breeze and his hat was set at a rakish angle, like Admiral Beatty's. He was having a swell time. The gentleman who was driving the car has been, since that night, a trifle stiff and distant with me. I suppose you can hardly blame him.

To go back to my daylight experiences with the naked eye, it was me, in case you have heard the story, who once killed fifteen white chickens with small stones. The poor beggars never had a chance. This happened many years ago when I was living at Jay, New York. I had a vegetable garden some seventy feet behind the house, and the lady of the house had asked me to keep an eye on it in my spare moments and to chase away any chickens from neighboring farms that came pecking around. One morning, getting up from my type-writer, I wandered out behind the house and saw that a flock of white chickens had invaded the garden. I had, to be sure, misplaced my glasses for the moment, but I could still see well enough to let the chickens have it with ammunition from a pile of stones that I kept handy for the purpose. Before I could be stopped, I had riddled all the tomato plants in the garden, over the tops of which the lady of the house had, the twilight before, placed newspapers and paper bags to ward off the effects of frost. It was one of the darker experiences of my dimmer hours.

Some day, I suppose, when the clouds are heavy and the rain is coming down and the pressure of realities is too great,

I shall deliberately take my glasses off and go wandering out into the streets. I daresay I may never be heard of again (I have always believed it was Ambrose Bierce's vision and not his whim that caused him to wander into oblivion). I imagine I'll have a remarkable time, wherever I end up.

JAMES THURBER

grew up in Columbus, Ohio, where he was born, and in time attended Ohio State University. There he edited the humorous undergraduate magazine. In his senior year he left college to do war duty as a code clerk in the State Department in Washington and later in the Paris Embassy. (He had lost the sight of one eye in a childhood bow-and-arrow accident and thus was incapacitated for active service.) After the war he became a newspaper reporter and worked variously on the Columbus Dispatch, *the* Paris Tribune, *and the* New York Evening Post.

In 1927 he joined the staff of The New Yorker *magazine. His first book,* IS SEX NECESSARY? *was written in collaboration with E. B. White, who was also a staff writer on* The New Yorker *at that time, and the book, illustrated with Thurber's drawings, was enormously successful. It marked the beginning of his literary reputation and his career as a humorous artist.*

Eventually he left The New Yorker *staff to devote his time to writing, although he remained a valuable contributor to the magazine. He is married to Helen Wismer, a former magazine editor and he lives much of the year in Cornwall, Connecticut. In spite of severely impaired eyesight, he has continued to create his matchless stories and drawings.*